MURPHY
WHO TALKS

First published in Great Britain in 2025
by Indie Novella Ltd.

INDIE NOVELLA www.indienovella.co.uk
Hackney, London

Copyright © Ronan O'Shea, 2025
The moral right of the author has been asserted.

All rights reserved. No part of this book may be reproduced in any form or by any electronic or mechanical means, including information storage and retrieval systems, without written permission from the author, except for the use of brief quotations in a book review.

All characters in this publication are fictitious and any resemblance to real persons, living or dead is purely coincidental.

A CIP catalogue record for this title is available from the
British Library
Paperback ISBN 978 1 918 16311 7

Printed and bound by in the United Kingdom.
Indie Novella is committed to a sustainable future for our readers and the world in which we live. All paper used are natural, renewable and sustainable products.

Indie Novella is grateful that our work is supported using public funding by Arts Council England.

MURPHY WHO TALKS

RONAN O'SHEA

For my mother and my father

Spring

Murphy Who Talks

Chapter One - March 2018

(4 Months Before)

- *Murphy tries in vain to warn a mouse*
- *Changes a Guinness barrel*
- *Explains loyalty to Mr. Handley*
- *Recalls how an avocado got him a job at The Purser's Retainer*

My name is Murphy, not to be confused with Murphy's, which is a stout from Cork. This was London, and I was in the cellar of The Purser's Retainer, changing a barrel of Guinness, which is from Dublin.

Names and places matter. Too much, sometimes, but they do all the same.

I was back in work, and that was good, and it was a job, and that was good too. It tempered thought. To some degree, I'd the peace and quiet in life I'd so long craved, though it was interrupted now as a mouse darted by my feet.

'G'wan Mickey,' I said, spirits lifted (I liked mice), then sunk, as I saw the direction it was headed; a green 'house' that would be its last. 'No, don't go that way.'

A snapping sound.

Mickey – or Minnie – had died so humans could eat and

drink safe in the knowledge that The Purser's Retainer followed Health & Safety regulations.

So it goes.

Moving on from his demise, I got on with the job, as the honest, hardworking barman is wont to do. There was a keg that needed changing, and so I was here doing that, freeing the Guinness nozzle from the keg, badly as it transpired.

'Ah!'

The red keg top shot up at me, a geyser of Guinness too, and I nearly died, maybe, or lost an eye. But all was well, I'd only a bit of Guinness on my white shirt. I stepped back, saw the strip light doused in the black stuff, and turned the gas off. I wiped the light. I'd made a fine mess of things. But it was okay.

It was also 13:32.

Before going back upstairs, I went to the gents to wash my hands. Looking in the mirror, I saw there was a bit of crisp between my teeth. I didn't like the teeth, asymmetrical, or the uneven Picasso eyes, or my chubby cheeks, but by and large, at The Purser's Retainer, I had found a place where I felt well within myself.

The Purser's got fewer customers than an ice cream van in December, which ought to have been cause for concern. But it'd been like that years, so who was I to question the system? Economics was never my thing, nor thinking ahead – too busy as I was with cluttered thoughts of then and now – for that matter.

I was getting by, and I'd no motivation to mess with that.

Back upstairs, I looked around my kingdom. It was good to be back in a bar, doling out joy, misery, solace and hope in equal measure, and whilst we didn't get many customers, those we

Murphy Who Talks

did we treated well. I wanted to keep it that way.

The pub sat on the Seven Sisters Road, opposite a building development called the Grayling Estate, where a flock of steel cranes were giving life to shiny, pricey flats that stared down at us with foreboding menace.

A rustling sound distracted me from my troubling thoughts, and I looked up to see Mr. Handley, the elderly regular – our only regular – who sat at the bar when he was in. He was reading a paper with his pint of Guinness.

Mr. Handley was a man of old-school views and modern complaints; positive discrimination and negative equity; migrant numbers and gender quotas; licence fees and student discounts. But now, it was his own discount which he'd issue with, namely the price of Guinness which he'd had to order, given his favourite – Pride – was currently off.

'It's utter rot, Murphy,' he said. 'The loyalty card should cover Guinness too.'

Mr. Handley had the Purser's loyalty card, but it only gave him a discount on ales, and Guinness is a stout, and terminology is important, so's to say what is that and this, this and that. I explained.

'Mr. Handley, sir, if we started discounting the Guinness, we'd have to do it with the Heineken, because the Heineken drinkers would be asking why you'd discount on Guinness and they didn't. We don't have many Heineken drinkers. Or many drinkers at all for that matter. But a point's a point.'

Mr. Handley buried his head in his hands.

'And then we'd have the Frontier lads kicking up a fuss,' I said. 'Then the cider drinkers, the pale ale army and–'

'Oh Christ,' said Mr. Handley.

'Well, now that you mention him, the wine lot might get involved and–'

'Murphy, enough twaddle.'

A pause, for Mr. Handley to settle into his frustration, and on I went, enjoying myself now, needling him for my own amusement.

'Mr. Nethercott–'

'Who?'

'Stephen Nethercott. The manager.'

'I know who he is, Murphy. Just call him Steve.'

'Mr. Nethercott has no say over the loyalty cards save for giving them out to loyal customers.'

'Isn't this a freehold?'

'No, it's part of a chain (a lie), it just has the look and feel of a freehold,' I said. 'Anyway. The discount is for ales alone and rules are rules. If we bend them for one, we've to bend them for all, and that leads to chaos. We can't be having that now.'

Mr. Handley sighed.

'But I'm only drinking Guinness because you don't have London Pride. And why is that?'

'Must apologise, sir,' I said. 'I have to admit that I forgot to tap the keg.'

Another sigh.

'And how long will it be until it's ready to drink?'

'Twenty-four hours, sir.'

'Is that the rule?'

'No, more a law of nature. It has to settle, otherwise it doesn't taste, well, like Pride.'

'And what is it that Pride tastes like?'

For effect, I even checked on the till.

'With the loyalty card it tastes like a £3.92 ale. Without, £4.53.'

He nodded. 'Sod off, Murphy.'

'Right you are, Mr. Handley.'

I went away. It was Monday, Mr. Handley the only customer, his white hair finely combed when he arrived but duck-like and messy now. I decided to clean the shelves.

It was 13:36.

I'd worked at the pub since November, which was typically a quiet month. December, typically busy, had been ominously quiet for us.

The world was in chaos, firms off *there* due to what was happening *here;* people slinging words at one another, arguments left, right, occasionally centre.

It felt as if there was a permanent noise, at all times, on the streets and in our minds, which would have been fine if some of that noise made its way into The Purser's revenue accounts. We were a ghost town, and much as I loved it that way, it didn't bode well.

It was a cold day when I first discovered the pub. I had been made redundant – more on this later – in January 2017. My mother had moved back to Ireland the previous month and, after a flying visit for my thirtieth birthday, I returned to find a badly paid job to do and an expensive flat to rent. I had found the flat. Next up was the job.

Walking, ruminating, crunching leaves, I saw a gorgeous, russet-coloured birch tree leaf, slightly out of the way. Moving towards it, I crunched, slipped and fell.

'Christ almighty,' I said, wincing with the pain.

My hands were cut, small pebbles embedded in purpling and bloodied skin. Moving the autumn leaves to see what had happened, I saw that someone had left a half-eaten avocado on the floor; the thinking man's banana.

Perplexed, I looked up and saw a pub in front of me: The Purser's Retainer.

The paint on the *r* – all of them – was cracked, and there was a sign in the window, which read:

Ronan O'Shea

Barman needed
Experienced preferred
Apply within

Barman?

I'd half a mind to inform the owner of the Equality Act of 2010.

But I also really needed a job, so I went in.

Equality could wait another day.

'Afternoon,' said the man behind the counter.

That was Stephen Nethercott. He'd whatever physical features you want him to have, and a blue and white striped shirt, well ironed. He had a soft, near- but not quite, posh, English accent, and a diabetic's bracelet.

'Hello,' I said. 'This is a nice pub.'

'Oh, thank you. You aren't from the area?'

'No,' I said, taking in the parquet floor, the red and green leather chairs, and the selection of red wines behind the bar, bigger than any pub I'd worked in before. 'But I live nearby.'

Stephen nodded.

'What would you like to drink?'

I would soon get to know Stephen well. He was taking on a barman to ease himself into early retirement and a gentler pace of life, not that running The Purser's Retainer was a particularly intense endeavour. He barely used the internet, read the physical papers, used a Nokia 3310, and had been the landlord (and owner) of The Purser's Retainer since the 1980s, possibly the only one in London not making a profit, healthy or otherwise.

That Nokia 3310 went off, buzzing on the oak counter. Stephen held a finger aloft, and I looked around his pub.

It was big, with many tables, stools and chairs, countless

drinks on tap and in fridges, and bottles behind the bar. There were drip trays, bar mats, glasses and plastic straws. It was behind the times.

In the cellar, there were gas canisters and kegs and boxes with wine, bottled beer and soft drinks and tonics, and there was a kitchen with a walk-in fridge where Chef made the food. Looking around, I spotted just two customers, and saw an opportunity: paid work, with minimal human interaction. The dream.

I'd to grasp it with both hands. At some point, I'd to clean those bloodied hands too.

The call ended.

'Sorry about that. What can I get for you?'

'I was keen on getting that job.'

'Do you have pub experience?'

'I do, both sides. But I never mix the two. I'm reliable, punctual and have a can-do attitude.'

'So, you can pour a pint?'

'Yes, I can do that.'

'What's your name?'

'Murphy.'

'Murphy, you have the job.'

He extended a hand.

'Can I use your bathroom?'

'Sure,' he said, hand still extended.

I showed – and explained to him – what had happened.

'Nasty graze,' he said. 'The toilets are downstairs.'

We never did shake on it, but I got the job in The Purser's Retainer all the same, and that's where I was shortly after the mouse's death, in March, when Stephen walked in with a mournful gaze in his eyes.

CHAPTER TWO

- *Murphy discovers what a Controlled Purchasing Order is*
- *Recalls the quixotic schemes that may have led to this point*
- *Comes up with a brilliant idea*

'Murphy, I have some bad news.'

'What is it, sir?' I said. 'Rise in oil prices? A run on the pound? Has Toys 'R' Us gone under?'

'No, no,' said Stephen. 'Well, actually, Toys 'R' Us went under a while back.'

'A crying shame. A huge pity, I'd say we ought to show solidarity with Toys 'R' Us. Give me a sec and I'll twee–'

'Murphy.'

His manner was pensive, bald pate sweaty. I sighed, resigned.

'You've no relatives you like left,' I said, which was true, his parents both gone, younger brother too, an elder estranged for reasons I'd not discovered. 'So I can only imagine you've the cancer, or it's about the pub.'

'It's about the pub.'

'Shit.'

Eyebrows lifted.

'I'm glad you don't have the cancer, Stephen,' I said. 'But

Murphy Who Talks

what is it, what's going to happen to the pub?'

'We've been given a CPO.'

'The droid fella from *Star Wars?*'

'Murphy, for one moment, be serious.'

It was like asking a chimpanzee not to fart and eat, sleep and screw.

'Murphy, we've been handed a compulsory purchase order.'

'What's that?'

Stephen pulled up a stool. Mr. Handley was sat at the other end of the bar.

'It's an order from the council, which forces us—'

I made a V with my eyebrows, such that he remembered I was on minimum wage, with no shares, and no stake other than the heart, soul and effort I put into the running and success (or lack thereof) of the pub.

'It forces me to sell.'

I could see Mr. Handley's ears pricking up.

'But can't you say no?'

'It's compulsory, Murphy.'

'I know, but the Democratic Republic of Congo is a 'democracy', the People's Republic of China a—'

'A tyranny. But this is Britain.'

I'd a nice little giggle as to the earnestness of that, and listened as Stephen went on to say words meant something here. Eventually, he stopped, giving me license to rant a while about my thoughts to the contrary, the hypocrisies of this and that and that and this, 'til eventually Stephen said, 'Shut up, Murphy', which I did, if only to let him explain what was going on.

Our local council, it transpired, had decided it was in the public interest that the land on which The Purser's Retainer sat be purchased by the developers currently building the Grayling Estate across the road. He went on, my Stephen, to say it'd been decided that this land be turned into facilities that would serve residents, residents who would 'regenerate' and 'breathe new life' into the area.

The profit thing, in short.

See, the Seven Sisters Road was deprived and it was poor, it was Muslim and it was black, too black to matter, most of the time. Between the lines, therefore, it was necessary to make this part of the Seven Sisters Road more lucratively staid, wealthy and white.

It was bad for the area, and it was goodnight Vienna for me, Stephen, and The Purser's Retainer, which would most likely become a Tesco Express or Morrisons local, a Prezzo or Honest Burger, Fitness First or Pure Gym, a Costa, Starbucks or Pret, or a Wholefoods for the busy city worker on the go, who worked hours too long to shop for more than ten minutes at a time. A temple of convenience for the money rich and time poor.

'Well, that's bad news,' I said. 'But it's not the end of the world.'

Stephen gave me a look, like pity.

'Erm, not for me, Murphy. I'm going to make a bit of cash out of this. But for you, well–'

'Oh, I'm not worried about the job,' I said. 'Worst comes to the worst, there are other places I can go, other pubs I can pour expensively priced–'

'Steady on.'

'Expensively priced drinks. *Because* London.'

'Ah.'

'But I don't want to work in another pub. I like it here. I like what we've done with the place.'

Stephen looked around the place.

'*We've* done nothing, Murphy. And I've barely changed a thing in two decades, except paint over the graffiti in the gents from time to time,' he said, which had varied over the years, I

Murphy Who Talks

knew; *Arsenal Invincibles 03-04*; *Vote Corbyn* (this was his neck of the woods); *Fuck Corbyn* (the bin collections could have been better); *No War in Iraq*; *Free Palestine* and, finally, *with every order* written beneath.

That last one was me, statement not political, only a reflection of my boredom on the day in question.

'That's the thing, Ste,' I said. 'That's what I like about it. Character. Tradition. History. But what I like and what's needed are a different kettle of cats altogether. It's not about me. It's about the pub. And by Christ's suspenders I don't want to see it close down, and I won't.'

I paused, for dramatic effect. If it had been a film, you'd have seen the vaguest hint of determination in my determinedly vacant eyes.

'I have a plan.'

Stephen looked worried, rightly so. I'd had plans before. The Purser's was a job, and it allowed me minimal interaction with customers. Save for Mr. Handley, who I'd quickly learned to give the *runaround*, I barely dealt with – and by proxy rubbed up against – anyone.

It was ideal, but nothing is perfect, and I'd known since the quiet of December that our days were numbered. There were no customers, little noise, few intrusions into the peace of my day. That was good. It was peaceful. But peace doesn't make money.

A compromise was needed.

I was tired of talking to people and tired more still of listening to them, but if I were to keep the job that minimised time spent doing both, I'd to boost numbers, and stop the pub closing down.

I'd had ideas before; Mystery Tap Tuesdays, the tubes swapped over downstairs, such that you'd order Amstel and get Guinness, or Guinness and get cider, if you see what I mean?

It was an unpopular failure.

I'd changed the décor, namely the artwork, shifting Stephen's Turner and Bacon landscapes, putting up portraits of obscure dictators and revolutionaries throughout the ages. Irony, like. It proved a controversial and offensive failure, the Albanian labourers from over the road taking exception to Enver Hoxha, the Croat lads agreeing that yes, Tito was a dictator but, benevolent, not so much.

I'd convinced Stephen to let the Christians use our space as a food bank, which brought in numbers, but not pounds, and Stephen cancelled the initiative after discovering I'd made myself a nice little supply line of donated, ground coffee that couldn't be given out to those in need for admin reasons, a mistake born of honest intentions, scout's promise.

Yes, I'd had bad ideas and given Stephen grounds for scepticism.

But the CPO called for desperate measures, out-of-the-box thinking and, of course, I had an idea.

'Stephen, if we turn this place around, we can show the council that the Purser's is an asset to the community.'

'But no one comes here.'

'That's what we've to change.'

'But no one will.'

'That's an attitude we have to change too.'

'And how are we going to do that, Murphy. Random taps? Dictator-chic decoration? Another sleep-in for Palestine, like the one that got us fined?'

'I admit I ought to have read up on the old health and safety,' I said. 'But with the student population up the road, it seemed like a sure-fire win.'

'Granted.'

'And how was I to know the Momentum lads would show

up in force?'

Stephen nodded.

'They really do come out of the woodwork when it comes to heavy drinking and having a pop at Israel.'

'Indeed.'

I nodded.

'Look. Times are desperate. The world's gone mad. We're being shut so they can turn this into a Leon, a Gail's or, if they get their way, yet more flats. We're going to play to our strengths, find our USP. Our personal brand.'

Stephen looked around the bar. Mr. Handley was reading his *Express*. You could hear cars driving past outside the window, the only other sound the hum of the fridges pumping out Co2 and the stark reality of our situation.

'All I hear from this place is the sound of silence, Murphy.'

I clicked my fingers.

'Exactly. That's our strength,' I said. 'Only we've to market it better.'

'What are you on about?'

'I'm saying we're going to advertise ourselves as *London's First Silent Pub*.'

'Silent?'

I put my fingers to my lips. He shook his head and said a thing he often did when he'd tired of me.

'Shut up, Murphy.'

I grinned.

'Now you're getting it.'

And that's how we became *London's First Silent Pub*, with capital letters, and italics besides.

It was 13:46.

The pub was dead, not even Mr. Handley here to darken our

doors; yet. The CPO was a crying shame. Ruminating on it, I went to the washing room, liberated a packet of crisps, read a message from my mother, and then various posts on social media.

I enjoyed Purple Hibiscus, thank you for sending it over. Darker than I expected. Too much war, not nearly enough flowers.

That was nice. The crisps and the posts less so. The crisps were too salty, the feeds sour, and there was toxicity in the air. I wanted to see The Purser's Retainer thrive, and I wanted to see the Grayling Estate suffer, but was there more to it than that?

I'd say so. I loved words. Indeed, they'd once been how I earned my pay; no longer. I had been an English teacher once, teaching people words they did not know, doing the same the following week when between they'd not bothered or not had time to practice what they'd studied. And I had been a journalist, or more of a content writer, churning out listicles and websticles and social media posts for pay, such that by the end of it I'd gotten to be jaded with the written word, what with them, unlike our pub, already dead and seemingly shorn of all meaning in the wider world.

Fake news
        Echo chambers
Saboteurs
    History as fantasy

                Reality as fallacy

      Hashtags as decency
THIS as solidarity.
        THESE TWO, community

Murphy Who Talks

Fools *threatened;* eejits who'd never had control demanding it back, encouraged by devious creeps who'd forever had it. Numbers on buses that belonged in dreams, adverts masquerading as the decency which belonged in the actions of women and men.

Yes, The Purser's Retainer had been a haven from it all, not least because Stephen barely knew how to work a touch-dial let alone a Twitter feed, so that we spoke *to* and *with* each other, mostly about stock orders and kegs, or whatever came to my mind, which riled him up fierce, and amused me no end.

I enjoyed the quiet, and the things I said to Stephen and Mr. Handley, the craic.

In the silence of the failing and near-empty bar I could avoid people's words, and revel in my own. The pub entertained me, gave me peace, handed me a wage and kept the chaos of the wider world at bay.

But it was dying on its arse, the root of its appeal presaging its demise.

We'd hardly any people, and no people meant the CPO, and the CPO meant no Purser's. But I'd found the answer.

London's First Silent Pub.

I had, in the strangest of places, discovered that within me, there was an untapped, entrepreneurial flair.

And that place was yoga, and I shall recount how that came about *right* now.

Chapter Three

- *Jackson Pollock, sneezing and the cancer*
- *How Murphy took up the yoga*
- *Of Gallic tax avoidance, sweaty rooms and a white boy's biases*
- *Delicious crème eggs*
- *The problem with bananas from Ecuador*

The waist was getting thicker, mind cloudier; I was in constant pain due to bad genes and worse mattresses.

Yoga, it was said, was good for back, bend, and soul.

It was a few weeks before Stephen's bad news.

I swung my feet out of bed and planted them on the floor.

It was 09:03.

Recently, I'd started sneezing profusely first thing in the morning, five or six times. A Welsh barman named Jim had once taught me a song.

Five is shit, six, well fine, seven near heaven but it's eight's divine.

Rumour had it eight sneezes caused orgasm. I only got to five. I reached for the tissues beside my bed, blew the old nose.

Murphy Who Talks

There was a knock on my door.

'Come in,' I said.

It was Juliette, lovely Juliette, my French housemate, clocking me as I clocked her clocking the tissues by my bed. A wave of horror shot through me, the thought of her thinking about me *here* with the tissues *there*. Revulsion, I imagined, running through her; a dark thought.

'You alright, Juliette?' I said in haste, to move things along.

'Yes, Marphy,' she said, all Gallic. 'Would you help me with my tax return? I do not understand the website.'

I had promised her I would.

'I will,' I said, 'In a jiffy.'

'What?'

'I'll be there in a minute.'

'Thank you.'

She left, the sneezes returned. Ach-oo, ach-oo, ach-oo I went, blowing my nose, worried by what I saw, a yellowish-brown-red coagulate, a Jackson Pollock in three-ply, a sign, for sure, that I had the cancer.

It was constant worry like this that had got me thinking I needed a solution. The Purser's Retainer had brought me much needed quiet, but not yet inner peace. I'd a good relationship with my clients (Mr. Handley, the occasional other) and boss, the days floated by, as did the cars outside the window, highlighting a steady decline that would soon land us the CPO. But my home life was another matter altogether.

I'd moved into the place in late-October, a third-floor flat on the Lorraine Estate in Holloway, the kitchen on the right as you walked in, two windows looking onto the Holloway Road and a dense bank of trees out front.

Dead ahead of the front door was Riyuichi's room, he a Master's student of Calisthenics at London Met, from

Hokkaido, Japan, who I never saw. To the left of his room was Juliette's and to the left of that mine, the pair of us side by side with only a thin wall in between. Juliette was quiet and, were it not for the occasional smoky cough, I wouldn't have known she was there.

At first, all was well. I'd found a place away from the noise outside; the shouts, the horns, the sirens.

But then, a couple of weeks in, I got a text from Juliette.

Murphy, please can you be more quiet in the mornings when you are walking around the apartment?

I felt like a fool. Me, noisy? I always tried not to be loud, out of place, a nuisance, *in the way.*

But clearly, I was failing; slamming doors, clattering pots into pans and pans into pots, dropping toiletries on tiled floors, knocking books into thin walls, clinking glasses on cups and plates on saucers, steaming the kettle, splashing water, buzzing my toothbrush, and banging about left, right and centre.

However, she only complained the one time. When I apologised, she wrote back *Ok*, and I'd no further issue. But still I worried, so I kept out of the flat as often as possible, on long walks. That's how I found the pub, and it's how I found yoga too.

It was late-February, a few weeks before I learned of the CPO or watched Mousie die. With a day off work, I grew restless in the flat, concerned that in making my lunch, pulling a book off my shelf, going to the toilet and everything in between, I might be disturbing Juliette, who was working in her room. So I went out for a long walk and decided to stop in for a takeaway coffee. As I waited for my flat white to be made, I saw a glossy flyer on the noticeboard:

Murphy Who Talks

Feeling:
Stressed out?
Worn out?
Strung out?
Run-down?
Love life D.O.A.?
TRY BIKRAM YOGA!

Juliette, I knew even then, was not the reason I left the flat so often. Yes, I liked walking in parks, chasing the squirrels, breathing London's fresh-ish air. But there was a restlessness to me, an anxiety of being within myself, and of being a burden on those around me. The Purser's brought me work, purpose, and a semblance of calm which dissolved the moment I returned home.

I had the answer: Eastern-infused calm, co-opted inner peace. I signed up, for a trial sum of £45 for thirty days, £75 thereafter.

The Yoga Studio's accountants loved me for it.

Back in my room, the Jackson Pollack-like tissue was a cause for concern. But the daily nature of the sneezes brought me comfort. The country didn't know if it was coming or going. My sneezes did.

Although I'd signed up to the yoga over a week earlier, I'd yet to go to a class; work having got in the way, hesitation and laziness too.

It was 9:43. Class was at 11:00.

I went to help Juliette with her tax, wondering if I'd have been so light of foot if she'd not been beautiful, if a male weakness in me explained my willingness to help her pay less tax.

I did it all the same.

'Thank you, Marphy,' she said, after I'd helped her figure

out the webpage.

'No bother,' I replied, returning to my room, packing my bag, heading to yoga for the first time.

'Have you been here before?'

'No.'

'Okay,' said the woman behind the desk, sat in front of a MacBook screen, beside an incense candle, beneath a row of yoga mats, for sale at twenty pound a pop. 'What's your name?'

'Murphy.'

'Aaand, first name?'

'Murphy.'

'Last name?'

'Murphy.'

The woman looked confused, the tribal tattoo on her wrist evidence of a zen-like worldview, an unfortunate experience in Bali, or both. 'You're called Murphy Murphy?'

I laughed. 'Absolutely not. That'd be mad. Just Murphy. Want to see my ID?'

She shrugged. 'No, it's fine. Here's a card. Beep it against the machine.'

I pressed the small black card against the scanner and said 'Beep beep'. It drowned out the beep. She asked me to do it again. I made no noise the second time.

'You can sit down,' she said, so I did.

It was 10:44. I was early. For a man of constant worry, maybe Bikram yoga wasn't a good idea. But here we were. Class began.

A hot room, baking even, with fifteen or so bodies. An instructor called Brenda, and two wall-length mirrors in front and to my side.

'Half-moon pose,' said Brenda.

She'd a purple and black Lycra onesie, a tattoo of the sun

MURPHY WHO TALKS

and moon, and another on her right arm inked in Sanskrit; peace, love, Haribo for all I knew.

I tried to follow what the others did, clasping, stretching, relaxing, bending, contracting. Whatever-*ing* Brenda instructed we do, I did, with limitations. The class had started with heavy breathing that had a Sanskrit name I don't recall; in, out, twenty times, knuckles beneath the chin, elbows raised to the air. Calming. It got harder after that, and I sweaty.

I slipped; I fell. I stood; I fell again.

'Very good, Murphy,' said Brenda, though eventually she told me to pause, to *take in* what the others were doing.

I watched. The mind wandered. Who were all these people? Why were they here? I watched others sweat, bend, stretch and exhale, and worried about the biases I had in me; what the black man next to me was most likely to do for a living, the personality of the blonde lady to my right, how much money and time the two women in their sixties had.

Despite fighting them, I'd biases still, and too many thoughts.

'And stretch, and stretch, and *stretch* one *more* time, said Brenda.'

As we stretched backwards towards the wall, I noticed there, when active, I wasn't thinking about it all; the biases, life in my own skin, the noise I made in the flat.

There, I thought only of stretching, not words, nor biases, nor worry, nor woe.

As soon as class was over, and I was walking home, thoughts crept back in. In Tesco, I bought a bunch of bananas at only £1.32, and knew someone in Ecuador was getting fucked over. But I needed, or wanted, bananas.

I bought a Creme Egg and tried not to think deeply about where the milk or sugar or chocolate came from, and thought back to the exertion in the hot, sweaty room; the mat on the floor, my concentration on mimicking the other people in the class.

It wasn't that I felt enlightened. No, I felt distracted, distracted and occupied. I decided I'd come back as often as I could.

The Purser's Retainer gave me respite from people, arguments, and the ever-growing noise of the outside world, while the flat, a haven from all those things, revealed the truth, that I was never fully at ease.

When I was at work, I found things to do; cleaning shelves, lifting barrels, winding up Mr. Handley. But now the pub was under threat.

I needed to bring customers to the pub, and I needed those customers to leave me alone, and the two rubbed up against one another like chalk and cheese.

The answer, of course, was silence.

Namaste.

Chapter Four

- *Murphy fights colonialism with crisps*
- *Avoids conflict by lying about his views on the EU*
- *Comes up with a thunderously good idea*
- *Bans the use of mobile phones, but not the phones themselves*

When I was at the yoga, I focused on the poses, and was calm, and when I was calm, I'd energy, a perverse inversion of why I'd taken up the yoga in the first place.

With energy came positive thinking, with that, ideas, good, bad, who's to say, but ideas all the same.

Radical change is easy on the ear but difficult to implement on the ground. Just look at the American Dream, the French Republic, Afghani democracy, or the introduction of VAR.

I was a cynic, but I was a dreamer too. At the core of most cynics is a desperately idealist heart. Or, if things have gone too far, the illusion of no heart at all.

I didn't believe in things. Religion, party politics, the hollowness of *causes*. The first seemed wonderful but unlikely, the second a replacement for the first. The last? To my mind, it was all too often co-opted by advertising or the whim of a news cycle.

I certainly did not believe in journalism, which was probably because I had tried my hand at it. If I were to believe in it, I would have to admit I had failed.

If I believed it were rotten to its core, I could believe it had failed me.

I had sat in newsrooms and seen the entitlement of liberal women and men as they dropped pieces of paper not into a bin but onto a floor, safe in the knowledge that the one brown face in the office would come and pick it up on their cleaning rounds. I'd had bosses ask me to rip off titles to whom we were supposed to be sat diametrically opposite, and I'd gotten all too used to doing my research not in the field but on the web, such was the post-decline of the digitally written word.

So it was fair to say I needed hope now, something to believe in. I might not have been able to save the English language, but I might at least save the place where people went to read it, speak it freely or, often enough, find refuge from those who use it with thoughtlessness, hate or stupidity.

Time heals all wounds or, at the very least, confuses us into submission. But time was something we hadn't the luxury of at The Purser's Retainer. We needed a revolution in the food and drinks industry, and fast. And we needed to change everything at the pub from the bottom up; the décor, the music, the Spanish expletives that drifted out to us from Chef, in the kitchen.

We also needed customers for who he'd a reason to cook food.

Yes, despite the cynicism I'd always been a dreamer, a fantasist even, but I'd tangible plans now, to turn things around. Yoga had given me a new energy, an understanding of strength in weakness. I was a man of worry, but a man of worry was a man of detail, and it was details that would save The Purser's

Murphy Who Talks

Retainer.

Starting with the crisps.

I walked back to the bar. Stephen was drinking lime cordial, reading *The Guardian*, Mr. Handley drinking Pride, reading his *Express*.

'Stephen,' I began. 'I've a capital id–'

Interrupted I was, by the old man, hitting the back of his hand against a right-wing paper.

'It's the EU,' said Mr. Handley. 'Telling them where they can fish, what they can fish. How to bloody *fish*.'

'Go fish,' I sighed.

'Shut up, Murphy,' said Mr. Handley.

'Yes, shut up Murphy,' said Stephen.

I looked at the pair of them, my mouth agape like a koi carp, eyes goggled and vacant like a trout.

'Sorry, Murphy,' said Stephen. 'Mr. Handley's throwing a wobbly about how the EU ruined UK fishing.'

Clearly, Stephen disagreed, as did I, because facts, like. But agreeing was no fun, so I took the devil's advocate line, to get the rise off my boss, and because he'd shut me up mid-sentence as I announced my plans.

'Tbf, Stephen, the EU has fishy previous in that regard,' I said, rambling a while about 'quotas' and such, and my old friend Per Hanssen, a 'lad I used to bartend with back in the day.'

'Oh, not now Murphy.'

'You see,' I went on. 'He'd a licence to fish in his father's lake, but the EU brought in new rules when the Scandinavian spotted black ling roe was declared threatened.'

'Scandinavian spotted what?'

'A freshwater fish. Goes well with celeriac mash and pea sauce, I'm told.' A Nissan Altima glided past the window. In this part of town. 'Anyway,' I went on. 'Per was fuming, said it was his only bit of peace after work on his dad's lumber yard. I told him to know his plaice. He neither got nor appreciated the joke.'

'Plaice is a seawater fish, Murphy,' said Mr. Handley.

I waved it away.

'Anyhow, Per was none too happy with the change, said it was a breach of rights. I told him 'Come on now, Per, rules are rules and fish are fish and if you've no rules in place you'd soon enough have no fish at all'. He didn't like that.'

Stephen sighed. Mr. Handley was the epitome of glee. Rumpled tweed too.

'What, if any, point are you trying to make, Murphy?' said Stephen.

'Long story short, he came to see that rules are rules and toed the line. Instead of fishing each day in his dad's pond he fished one there Monday, two on Tuesday, and so on in his neighbours' ponds the rest of the week.'

'Where did you say this lad was from?'

'Sweden,' I said. 'Östersund.' I scratched my head, feigning remembrance of a different lad altogether. 'No wait. That wasn't Per Hanssen of Östersund. We did e-bike tours in Athens together. Things ended badly for him. I'm thinking of my old friend Artiom, Moldovan lad.'

'Who was living in Sweden?'

'No, on his father's beetroot plantation in Moldova, an hour west of Tiraspol. Was only in Greece a few months for a change of scene.'

Stephen furrowed his brow. 'Moldova isn't in the EU.'

I laughed, 'remembering' myself. 'What a prize elephant I am.'

'An idiot.'

'A fish-brained fool.'

Murphy Who Talks

'Refill my cordial, Murphy,' said Stephen. 'And then please do go away.'

'Cordially glad to, so.'

I filled his glass, glad to have gotten the rise off him after he'd shut me up so, went to the backroom, unlocked my phone, and read a message from my Mum as I sipped on Coca-Cola post-mix and water poured from the tap.

I'm after being ticked off by the guards, she'd written, a surprise, as in my lifetime she'd had no run-in with the law.

What for? was my reply, anticipation bubbling in me, as the one-tick grey turned two tick-grey, but not blue, 'til finally it did, *Vandalism* the response, the word a surprise, her use of a full stop not. Mum, a stickler for rules.

Vandalism?

Yes, I was tidying up the shop fronts, wrote Mum, relaying how since moving home she'd noticed a *shocking* trend in the town where she was born; sturdy, solid fonts, piss-poor punctuation; a death of possessives on shop windows. There was *Peggys* not *Peggy's*, *The Friends Café*, *Kids Corner* and *Mrs. Teas Bakery*, my mother as put out by the '.' after *Mrs* as she was by the missing ''' after *Tea*.

Rules are rules.

So you took matters into your own hands? was the rhetorical query my end.

Yes, her reply, *fair play* mine.

Further enquiry revealed that my mother (who'd only moved back to her hometown of Cashel, Tipperary, in December 2016) had hit the ground running as a local oddball and scourge.

When I was a young child, she had been a nurse; during my adolescence, she had retrained as a librarian, and now, she was nursing grammar; a linguistic pedant, Florence Nightingale with a Sharpie in hand. Retired and bored, she had, quite clearly, gone mad.

And I loved her for it.

She'd gone into the town centre with her Sharpie, a step ladder and a determined gait, and altered the signs so they adhered to linguistic rather than current norms. The shop owners were left scratching their heads, the guards dumbfounded, Mum rewarded with a stern talking to, and a €100 fine.

It was worth it, her summary.

Brilliant stuff, my reply, with capitals, to honour the fact that my love of words and each meaningless, pedantic act of defiance I'd ever committed – or would commit – was borne of her influence.

Sometimes, when the chips are down, the world in chaos, society against you and current trends ahead, you have to take matters into your own hands. I wasn't going to let Stephen silence me, at least not twice in one day. I put my phone away, and went front-of-house to tell him how I was going to fix his pub.

'Stephen, these have to go.'

I held up a packet of Jackson's crisps, the little Union Jack in the right-hand corner glaring up at me, the *sea salt* and *crushed pepper* an elaborate marketing joke like the fin de siècle, nautical vignette on the front, a port of sorts, so very historic, twee and English.

Two could play at that game.

'The crisps?'

'Aye, the crisps,' I said.

'I like those crisps,' said Mr. Handley.

'Mr. Handley likes those crisps.'

All the better.

'Mr. Handley likes gone-off Pride and capital punishment,' I said.

Murphy Who Talks

'Are you saying the Pride is—'

'Our Pride is *not* go—'

'Gentlemen,' I said, raising my hands in the air. 'A pub's only as good as its crisps. And these represent a dark, imperialist chapter in our history. They're borderline racist.'

Mr. Handley let out an 'Oh Christ'. Stephen asked me what 'the hell' I was harping on about. I pointed to the Union Jack with its imperialist undertow and the galleon ship its oppressive, colonial associations.

'We're getting rid of these crisps. We're going to be more inclusive, discard these colonial throwbacks, replace them with something both neutral and delicious, which can be enjoyed by everyone.'

'And what's that, Walkers?'

I shook my head. 'No, folks. We're going to bulk-buy Taytos.'

And so it began.

Taytos. The best crisps there are.

I knew my biases, knew if I was to suggest change to Stephen it had to be evidenced based.

I had taste-tested wide and far; Quavers, Walkers, Doritos, Kettle Chips, The Crisp Co. I'd tried them all so as not to let shamrock-tinted nostalgia cloud my judgement, blinkered as it could be with memories of the annual pilgrimage *home*, the free and heady days of youth.

Taytos were as Irish as cousins in America and red lemonade, framed pictures of JP2, Christ One and the Virgin Mary staring down from gaudily papered walls; mass on Sunday, Galtee cheese, Mikados, Lotto, Guinness, Sharon Corr, Daniel O'Donnell, the Sam Maguire, Jack Charlton (honorary), Swift (purloined), Joyce (prodigal), O'Connell, Connolly, the harp and the pint of Harp too.

If you were to post a card from that place the English always promised to go but never did (France is warm, Spain too) a packet of Taytos with a Queen-free stamp was as good as Guinness is Good For You, an aul' fella outside a pub, a sheep dicking around on an infertile, green hill.

'But people like Jacksons crisps,' said Stephen, eyes on the bag in my hand.

'Look around you, Stephen.'

He did.

'Granted.'

'We've to be ambitious,' I said. 'Think big. Start small. Own your crisp game.'

Stephen paused for thought. 'What's that word you use to describe idiots, Murphy?'

'Idiots?'

'No, you had another word you use, time and again.'

'Elephants?'

'No, no, no,' he said, hand waved in irritation. 'Something el–'

'Lutes. Fools. Prize pineapples, numpties, weapons, tools, eejits, baboo–'

'Eejits! That's it. Eejits.'

'What about them?'

'You are an eejit, Murphy.'

'A first-rate fish's tit,' I said. 'But will you give the Tayto notion a chance?'

To my surprise, he did. And so, we became the *first English pub to serve Taytos* (not that I checked) up and down the land.

It was a victory over the Island and a small act of defiance. English history was largely a lie; the flag could do one too.

But why had I such an antipathy for the land of my birth?

I was what's known as Plastic; English born, Irish by way

of identity; try-hards with London accents. I was born in Barnet, a few miles north of Holloway, thirty-one years earlier. Mum was Eileen, father John. My older brother was named after him, older sister her. By the time I came around, they were out of ideas.

Hence Murphy.

My brother is a banker in Dublin, my sister a lecturer at Glasgow University, and the world's foremost expert on the sex life of clownfish. Go fish.

Eileen Snr. first came to London in 1975, moved there in '77. She spoke about it on occasion but never in full, never *with* or *to* us and certainly never all of us at the same time.

John arrived in 1976, met my mother, and they stayed. They married in 1979.

He was a sailor, Eileen a nurse, he from west Kerry, she Tipperary. They settled in North London.

She nursed the old in hospital and the young, in us, while he sailed; coming and going, over and over, ferrying Maersk containers full of God knows what from here to there and everywhere in between, earning, living, missing, praying, sleeping, sailing.

'til 1991, when he died. Lost at sea.

After which it was just the siblings, me and Mum.

It was 14:46.

'Ha! Look at this Murphy.'

I walked over. 'What's that now?'

'It's going to be warmer in England than in Portugal this weekend. By jove.'

He was borderline ecstatic. Mr. Handley loved it when England was hotter than places, particularly if they were hot places. I didn't know if this was because he disliked hot places, *other* places, both, or if he had in him a FOMO that manifested itself in distaste.

He had been at the pub every day since I began, and I had the impression he didn't get away from England much, hadn't since hitting his sixties and, like many an elderly racist, gave equal room in his mind to all things foreign as he did sources of fibre, knife crime and the supposed benefits of No Deal.

He was a character, regular and pain in the arse; a blight on my ears and me on his, and despite it all, I liked him.

But he was also the only real disruption to my peace, his contrarian views a challenge, such that I'd to give him the *runaround* wherever possible so only as to keep myself sane.

'Have you ever been to Portugal?' I said. 'It's a lovely place.'

Mr. Handley shook his head.

'The Portuguese did themselves a mischief in that recession,' he said, leafing to the next page, the story that had got him so excited already old news. 'Erratic people.'

'Oh no,' I replied. 'I once knew a lad from Alentejo, in the south of the country. Very smart.'

Mr. Handley lifted an eyebrow, as if to say he'd give me the time, if not much of it, and only sparingly.

'Ran a farm out in the back of beyond, small villa with goats, sheep, cows and a few rabbits. He'd studied business in London, Keynesian economics in Paris and had a PhD in SEO marketing that he'd got at a university in Aarhus.'

'Why there?'

'Bursary.'

He sneered, muttered something about 'hand outs' and the conversation went on.

'He ended up going back to his parents' farm, and you know what he did? He took the goats that had been doing little and the sheep ponderous, and made goats and sheep's milk, branded it organic and artisan, and made himself a tidy little fortune besides. No, not erratic at all, Mr. Handley, very

Murphy Who Talks

clever.'

'And you knew this chap?'

'I did yes, I met him while I was working as an English teacher at a language school in Spain.'

'He was teaching Spanish?'

'No, I think he was a Portuguese teacher,' I said, placing two glass bottles in the fridge. 'Smart lad.'

'He was in Spain, teaching Portuguese to Spanish people?'

'To the Dutch, the English, the French. Sometimes the Spanish too. Though the bulk of his income came from café work. He used to serve me coffee in a small bodega just off Calle Alfalfa, though if I'm honest, I usually ordered red wine.

'If he was so smart, what was he doing working in a Spanish café?'

I sighed. Mr. Handley had on him a view that all Portuguese were the same; erratic, spendthrift and mercurial, that a man behind a café counter must be a man who's made bad choices, not a man whose country has forced drastic choices or no choices upon him.

'His wife was from the city,' I said.

It was a lie, of course, but appeased Mr. Handley. Still, I couldn't resist getting the rise off him.

'And look at me, Mr. Handley,' I said. 'We're not all lutes and fools, us who serve. There's more to us than meets the eye.'

Mr. Handley smiled. 'You, Murphy, are a fool.'

'A weapons-grade numpty, sir. Would you like another drink?'

'Yes.'

I poured Mr. Handley another beer, took his money, went to the back room, and ate a packet of crisps.

My beef with England wasn't that it was in a state of chaos or had lost the run of itself, both of which were true. It wasn't that the state had failed its people, even people as old as Mr. Handley, who'd nary a clue as to what is the what and how the how; true also.

It was the seriousness with which it carried itself. An utter lack of fun. England had stopped being *funny*. England.

Yet I still lived here, still had hope, unlike Mum, who had moved home decades after she had first moved to London. She had bought a small two-up, two-down on the outskirts of Cashel, opting for green fields and rural calm, extortionate healthcare and a different kind of neoliberal government who saw the poor as very much the same scum.

Her moving home was a surprise. It was me, not my mother, who spoke so fondly of Ireland; me who'd never lived there, learned there, loved there, lost there. But it was she who'd gone back.

Her reason, she said, was that she'd 'never felt so uncomfortable here', a little excessive to my mind.

When she arrived, the Irish were suspected Semtex-enthusiasts; now, we basically ran the BBC, were white enough to edit newspapers, and our children could even head the EDL.

We'd come far.

So, Mum moved, and I stayed. For all its flaws, England was my home, and though I didn't like chaos, a part of me wanted to hang around to see how things would pan out.

And then I lost my job. Having floated around London's freelance journalism scene (a lonely, sadomasochistic domain, without the physical pleasures), I was by this point a salaried sub-editor on an in-flight magazine. Or had been. No longer. Now, uncertainty reigned supreme once again, and on that morning when fate dictated I fall over, scrape my knee, and look up to see Stephen's job ad, I found purpose, endeavour, and a way to hide from the same chaos my mother tried to escape.

The pub had saved me and, even in spite of Mr. Handley and his views, I wanted to save it. I wanted the good ship Purser to change its worn-out, tiresome image, and I wanted to beat the bastards up at the Grayling Estate, who hoovered up my city the way an anteater does ants. I wanted to be of use.

I was tired of short-term answers, gimmicks, slogans, depthless ideas. It would take more than Tayto crisps to change the image of our pub.

It was 14:50.

It was 16:03.

Mr. Handley had gone home. Stephen was back out front, whiling away the time with the Guardian crossword.

'Stephen,' I said. 'Remember I was talking about silence?'

'Vaguely. You wanted to make it our USP, I recall. But then you got distracted by a so-so brand of crisps.'

For the sake of his business, I let it slide.

'...'

'Okay, a superior brand of crisps.'

I guess, in my silence, I didn't let it slide.

'Thank you,' I said.

'What about silence, Murphy?'

'People love their phones.'

'Erm, yes. They do, Murphy.'

'But they love a fad.'

'Uh huh.'

'And the only thing people love more than a fad is being *in* on one.'

'Go on.'

So I did.

'If we were the only pub in the area that banned the *use* of mobile phones, we'd be the talk of the town.'

A police car floated past outside, sirens off. Stephen looked confused.

'Isn't the whole social media thing about word-of-mouth?' he said, asking then how we'd get publicity if people couldn't 'facebook' and 'tweet' and 'snap that' about these things.

I'd a nice little giggle at that.

'Snap*chat*, Stephen.'

A kid with a basketball bounce, bounce, bounced a ball past the front door and windows.

'You're right,' I said. 'They do. And they will. If they can't use their phones *inside*, they will *outside*. We'll be the sort of place you need to see to believe. Like Disney. Or Stevenage.'

I had his attention, was as surprised as anyone by the fact.

'So, we're going to ban phones?'

'No,' I said. 'We're not going to ban anything. Never works. Look at drugs.'

He nodded.

'Except noise. We'll eventually ban that. That'll work.'

'Why?'

'It just will.'

'Okay,' said Stephen. 'About the phones?'

I paused, for effect, like.

'Right, the phones. We're not going to ban them. But we are going to proscribe *the use* of them.'

'I don't understand.'

'That's probably an advantage.'

'Right,' he said. 'Wrap it up, Murphy. I have a hair appointment at–'

I looked at him a certain way.

'Don't look at me that way, he said, and in fairness he'd a slight, fuzzy carpet-like thing at the back and sides.'

'Apologies,' I said. 'Before we ban noise, we've to acclimatise people. We'll start with the crisps, move on to the phones, and then have an outright ban on words.'

'I thought you said banning things didn't work?'

'I never said that,' I said, and with Stephen rightfully set on telling me that I had, I went on to say we'd to ultimately mark ourselves out as 'unique' and 'different' and 'trendy' and whatnot.

'It's brand building, Stephen. A new way of business. Quirky.'

He sighed. 'Quirky is the last thing I want to be, Murphy.'

'What about poor?'

'I am poor.'

'No, you're broke. There's a difference.'

He sniffed the air, conceding.

'Of course, eventually, we *will* ban people from talking,' I said. 'But you have to do these things incrementally. I call it *goalpost creep*.'

'What's that when it's at home?'

'A gradual, subtle but inalienable shift in the state of play that has you wondering where it will end and how in hell it began.'

He nodded. 'And you want to do this by stopping people from using their phones?'

I smiled.

'I like the way you didn't use the word ban. You're a natural, Stephen.'

He frowned.

'Okay, Murphy. I'm bored, my back aches, I've had rather too much cordial for one day, and I can't for the life of me remember the capital of Alaska,' he said, looking down at a crossword, a pen in his hand now abeyant. 'We'll try things your way.'

And that's how we became the first pub in the country not

to ban mobile phones, only the *use* of them.

Was it a good idea? Probably not. Was my small act of defiance against colonialism futile? Probably, but it also meant I could eat the crisps I liked. Did I, even back then, think it would end in anything other than stunning failure? Who knows? I can't remember every thought that crossed my mind, though I did know I was doing everything I could to get a bit of peace in the bar (I *was* banning phones, and I was doing it to curtail myself as much as any other), and I knew the capital of Alaska besides.

'Six letters?'

'Yes.'

'Juneau.'

And that's how Stephen discovered the capital city of Alaska.

It was 16:08.

Chapter Five

- *Murphy and Mr. Handley argue over the mobile-phone usage ban*
- *Murphy bribes Mr. Handley*
- *Stephen discovers the dark sectarianism behind Murphy's crisp obsession*
- *Murphy lures in the British media with his nose for a faddy trend*

It was 13:00.

The mobile-phone initiative had proved an instant success, a raft of new customers coming and going through the doors. We'd bought a safe where they could store their phones. They did so with glee but, without fail, I'd to inform them not to photograph the act. They felt denied and disappointed, unsure what to do with themselves, a phenomenon to which I'd soon find a solution. In the interim, they were told that they didn't have to use the safe, but nor could they use their phones.

The rules were rules, and they were clear.

Mr. Handley did not agree.

'Now sir,' I said to him, during the umpteenth protest. 'We've publicans' rights to refuse service to anyone we see fit to, as it is. Your custom is valued here, but not *this* custom.'

'What custom?'

'You know, the tapping, the texting, the phoning, the sexting. Not in your case, of course.'

'What is se—'

'What I'm saying is, we've instigated the no-phone policy and there's no wriggle room to manoeuvre on the matters of the fact. Rules are rules, Mr. Handley, they're to be followed and observed.'

A sigh, backdropped by a passing car out of the window, a Volvo Elastica I believe.

'But it's *your* rule, Murphy,' he said, palms in the air. 'Why don't you just drop it?'

'Because it's going to change things round here,' I said, looking around the pub.

It was mid-afternoon. We'd unfamiliars, tourists even, and Chef was busy in the kitchen making food served not with the little Union Jack on a cocktail stick as before, but an EU flag, so only as to wind Mr. Handley up. He was sat there now, asking why I was punishing him so.

'But the rules must apply to regulars too,' I said. 'You'll get no special treatment here. The Purser's Retainer is a place of refuge, a socialist utopia. A round table with a straight bar.'

'I want nothing to do with socialist utopia,' said Mr. Handley, the missing article purposeful, his fear of Marxism clear, the air punctuated with light chatter, the tinny tinkle of Chef's Bolivian lo-fi trance in the kitchen, and the passing of cars on the Seven Sisters Road.

Mr. Handley wasn't best pleased.

'Where in blazes is Stephen?' he said. 'I want to talk to him about this phone nonsense.'

A smile off me, the needle sharpened. 'He went to the bank,' I said. 'Have you got his number? I'm sure he'd be glad to take your call.'

Murphy Who Talks

Mr. Handley took out his phone, Nokia 3310 just like Stephen's. I wagged my finger, grinning behind the eyes.

'What?'

'Not in here, Mr. Handley.'

A scowl.

'Shut up, Murphy.'

And a grumpy old man, tottering off his stool and out of the pub.

Mr. Handley's complaints aside, the mobile-phone policy had gone down well. The pub was attracting custom. Building work was of course still going on over the road, but the more heads we had coming through the door, the greater our chances of demonstrating to the council the vital social role The Purser's Retainer played in the local community. And if that didn't work, we could show them the profit margins.

I felt more peace at home, when I was there, my shifts having doubled as I led the initiative from the front, albeit on the same rate of pay.

All the same, I was lighter; I worried less about noise, gliding around with grace. In letting go of my fears, it seemed I'd stopped doing the things that caused them, the bumping, stamping and clattering that'd led to Juliette's reproach before.

But the initiative with the phones had led to customers, and the customers to more noise, and so my peace was disturbed. The pub was busier, I'd to work more hours, had less time for yoga, and only had myself to blame.

Why?

I had sent the following email to an old editor of mine. Words, once my source of pay, had eluded me in over a year. The WhatsApp aside, I'd not written a-one, yet here I was, dipping my toes into the written word again, via email.

Ronan O'Shea

Hold the Lines
A look inside London's first mobile phone free pub

Hi, Glen, how are you? As you know I'm not in the writing game now, but I've come across an unusual pub called The Purser's Retainer. I figured you might be keen to add to your ken, Glen.

I didn't mention that I worked at the pub, said only I'd *come across* it, explained the pub had banned not phones but only their use, and that we'd a large safekeeping safe by the door.

'Seems a bit excessive, doesn't it?' Stephen had asked, when I mooted the safe idea.

'Ambition always does.'

'Stands out a bit, no?'

'See above,' I said, though as we were speaking, not reading, he'd to think a second before two and two paired up.

'Ambition aside, won't it look a bit out of place here?' said Stephen, pointing around himself, at the old oaken bar, the traditional furnishings, the distinctly unoffice-like atmosphere of the place.

'Stephen. You said so yourself, this pub is dying a death.'

'I didn't quite use those words.'

'Close enough. Now's the time to be bold. To shake things up a bit. To play with the mainframe.'

Mr. Handley, still grumbling but abiding by the rules, rifled through his copy of the *Express*.

'Murphy, what are you wittering on about?' said Stephen.

'Big plans call for a big safe. Big ideas, bold thinking.'

A pair of eyebrows, Stephen's, rising and falling like the moon.

'If I buy it,' he said. 'Will you stop wittering on?'

'Certainly sir,' I said. 'At least for now.'

Murphy Who Talks

And so the safe was bought. Its code was 1976, the year The Clash brought out *The Clash*, which was good, as me and Stephen wouldn't forget it, Mr. Handley wouldn't have a clue. And in between it all, Glen Simmonds had replied.

Hi Murphy,
Good to hear from you, how are things these days?

And then:

This sounds insane!!

The *!* and the *!* needled me, but I was glad to see I'd piqued his interest. He asked me for more details, how I'd discovered the place, at which point I confided that I did in fact work there now.

I had him hook, line and sinker. He said he'd send a writer down, and while I was tempted to say *I'm* a writer it was now true I was not.

I was a barman, and that was fine, good, grand even. Perhaps.

Stephen would be interviewed by the magazine, Mr. Handley too, after we bribed him with a week's worth of Pride.

That was mid-April.

We were now in the full throes of May, with its blossoming cherry trees, mercurial weather and the bastard promise of hay fever. With pollen in our nostrils and dreams in our hearts, we'd set out on an ambitious project for a quiet pub across the street from a noisy building site on the Seven Sisters Road, to draw the punters in by giving back to them what they had always wanted: the traditional English pub, albeit with post-colonial crisps.

And they loved us for it.

The feature was out, my grinning Celtic rictus on the front page. The majority of the photos were of punters talking to each other over half pints of lager in ornate thistle glasses, the rest of yours truly; pouring those half pints, serving the gobshite from the magazine, another of me with fingers to lips, an inaudible *shhh* without the *!*

Mr. Handley was quietly pleased, gazing at his photo in print as a man in a zoo, stroking the page, a glint of something in his eye; a sense of inclusion maybe, which he sat with a moment before laughing maniacally and saying 'What a hoot Murphy, you fool'.

Order restored, vulnerability bulwarked behind a smoky laugh and one of his many free pints.

Customers came in droves to see what this mobile-phone free pub was all about; a few builders in orange Hi-Vis from the site, but mostly beard-twiddling hipsters delighting at the novelty of it all as they put their mobiles in the safe – and our care – before buying their drinks, sitting down, disappointed they couldn't document their night out, such that it might as well not have happened at all.

How do you capture the moment when the tools are locked up in a safe?

I'd an idea.

'They don't know what to do with themselves,' said Stephen, in the early days, seeing them marvel at the Retainer's traditional furniture; the kitsch horse and hound photos restored to the bar in lieu of Stalin, Mao and the like.

'Analogue, Stephen. We'll go analogue.'

'What?'

'Polaroids. People love Polaroids.'

'I haven't seen a polaroid since the mid-80s.'

MURPHY WHO TALKS

'And do you look back on the mid-80s fondly?'

'I do.'

'Because you were young, all was ahead, the times were better?'

'No, because I had a wife. And hair.'

'The promise of youth,' I went on. 'The antithesis of the modern age. Click click, print print. This lot will eat it up, mark my words.'

'Murphy, the only thing I want of your words is their end. Do whatever it is you have planned and get on with it.'

And so I bought two polaroid cameras, and several reams of film, convinced it would aid our well-meaning fad hunters in their experiential goal. Stephen baulked when I told him the whole set up had cost close to a hundred and fifty of his pounds.

'Jesus Murphy, we're bleeding money.'

'No, we're bleeding humans,' I said. 'But money makes of us utt–'

'Enough,' said Stephen. 'How are we going to make money if you keep spending it?'

It was the crisps, I said; the change from Jacksons to Taytos was after – I was sure – boosting our fortunes.

'Stephen, with the money we've coming in off the Taytos, the film and cameras are a pittance.'

He sighed. 'We're making less money on the new crisps than we were on the old,' he said, to which I said 'WTF', though knowing he'd not understand what I was talking about added 'What the actual fuck, Stephen?'

'It's true,' Murphy, he said. 'They're not shifting.'

'Let me take a look.'

I walked into the washer room, realised the mistake I'd made, and walked back out.

'I'm an utter giraffe, Stephen,' I said.

He'd no grace to say *No, Murphy, you're not*, and asked instead, 'Why?'

I held a blue pack of Salt & Vinegar Taytos in the air, like a used rubber. 'These crisps are from the North.'

'What are you talking about, Murphy?'

I'd let trust get the better of me. My contact from Roscommon had let me down. When I thought on it, it was possible he'd travelled North to buy the crisps cheap and brought them South to sell on, though if you were to ask me if Taytos from the North were cheaper or more expensive than their equivalents from the South, I'd not be able to answer honestly; could only tell you that at that time at least, there were no border checks to ensure nobody was shifting Taytos between nations hidden in car boots, thereby making them cross-border potato-based contraband.

I'd no idea of anything, at all.

'These crisps are from the North, Stephen,' I said.

'Like, Manchester?'

'No. *The* North. Red Hand. Gorgeous Georgie Best. Aldi-quality country music. Himself Ian Paisley. The Titanic. Norn Iron. *Northern*. Ireland.'

'What does that matter?'

I sighed.

'Taytos from the North are not the same as Taytos from the South. They look the same, but they aren't the same, see?'

'No.'

Was it ever thus? I sighed again, ashamed of what I'd to tell him. What I was about to say was morally wrong but factually true, and the future of The Purser's Retainer depended on it.

'Protestants can't make crisps, Stephen.'

A look of bafflement.

'I know it's not easy to understand.'

Murphy Who Talks

The look unchanged.

'I don't know why,' I said. 'I've no idea how it came to pass, know only that the best quality Taytos are made south of the border, in Erin. Something in the grass, or water I'd say.'

The look finally changed.

'You don't half talk some twaddle, Murphy.'

A holy trinity of sighs, the poor man understandably confused, wrong and right, right and wrong, but on this matter, more one than the other.

'Absolutely, sir,' I said. 'Worse than Mikael Koskinen, a Finnish lad I once knew who could never end a sentence he was so busy talking.'

Stephen's patience, visibly wearing thin, while in the background a hipster lad was talking about an upcoming Marvel retelling of *Seven Samurai*, with Ben Affleck feted to appear, God forbid.

'I've no clue as to why,' I said. 'But I know the what, and the what is that southern Taytos are the bee's knees, the badger's nadgers, the real McCoy, you might say, were it not a crisp-based conversation that'd lead you to thinking of McCoy's, a competitor brand.'

'Get to the point.'

'The point is my contact from Roscommon has let you, me and, most of all, himself down. But all is not lost. Fortunately, I get my own supply from elsewhere, and I'll sort it out.'

'Okey dokey, Murphy. Can I go now?'

'Yes.'

'Good.'

And it was good. What was less good, in a nostalgic sense, is that Mr. Handley was now so fed up of my rules are rules lark that he'd told me that he was going to start drinking in The Orang-utan's Bazaar, a rival pub.

'The grass isn't greener on the other side, Mr. Handley.'

'How would you know, you fool?' he said. 'You're just a child.'

It was a fair point, but false. I knew.

And I will – briefly – tell you why, as I did him, *right* now.

Chapter Six

- *Murphy explains why the grass isn't always greener on the other side*
- *Murphy remembers Prague*
- *Mr. Handley listens*
- *Murphy has hope*

It was 13:14.

'Another Pride before you leave us, Mr. Handley?' I asked.

'Fine.'

Despite his forthcoming treachery, I gave him the loyalty-card price.

'Trying to butter me up, Murphy?'

'Turning the other cheek.'

'Christ almighty.'

'The very one.'

'Get on with your story.'

It was 13:15.

'The summer of 2008. A bastard of a year,' I said, serving the man a russet-coloured pint. 'My Uncle Billy was in hospital. The kidney stones.'

'Ach.'

'And he'd coeliac disease.'

'The no-gluten business?'

'The very one,' I said, said too it was alright in the end, he was 'out before you knew it', then came to 'stay with us for a few weeks', and added – for *runaround* purposes – that he came for 'a bit of peace and quiet'.

'With you?' asked Mr. Handley, taking his first sip, as a Škoda Tomcat shot through the lights out front.

'Beggars can't...'

He nodded. I went on.

'So, Billy's staying with us a few weeks and, at this time, mum's working long hours, seven-thirty 'til six.'

'Right. She was a nurse?'

'Had been. She was a librarian by this time.'

Mr. Handley looked at me queer.

'There's a lot of books to shelve during the summer period,' I said. 'Make hay while the sun shines.'

Mr. Handley nodded, asked me why I 'wasn't working' myself, to which I said, 'I was. Nights. Volunteering at the condom factory on a purely pro boner basis.'

Bawdy, it got a laugh off old Mr. Handley.

Truth be told, I had been a barman at the time.

Stephen, meanwhile, was at the other side of the bar, holding a Tayto in the air like communion bread, as if looking at it would reveal the flaw that meant we'd crisps from the wrong side of the border.

I continued, told Mr. Handley about Uncle Billy convalescing at 'our place', and how I made his breakfast each day; gluten-free porridge with raisins and dates, occasionally a banana, a few nuts the one time.

'So? You did your familial duty,' said Mr. Handley. 'What's it got to do with me going to another pub? Why should your mother have had to bear the brunt of looking after him?'

Murphy Who Talks

I peered out of the window, towards the street.
'Odd.'
'What?'
'Hell's not frozen over,' I said. 'Yet here we are, in agreement for once.'
His face soured. 'Shut up, Murphy.'
I smiled.
'Right-oh.'
'And get on with it.'
So I did.
It was 13:16.

'You're right, Mr. Handley. Had my mother been free I'd have done my duty all the same, though what matters is that Mum wasn't working all those early mornings, the way she said she was.'
'No?'
'No,' I said. 'That was a lie.'
'From you?'
'From her.'
'Ah. I assumed–'
I held my hand up. 'I've given you reason to doubt, on the *odd* occasion.'
Mr. Handley took another sip, asked me what Mum was up to if she wasn't working.
'No idea,' I said. 'Reading books in cafés, going for a drive. Who knows? All I know is she did it to get me out of bed. I'd taken to sleeping in.'
'Because you were a lazy student?'
'No, Mr. Handley. Because I was depressed.'
I mopped up a bit of spilled ale so I wouldn't have to look him in the eye.
'How'd she know?' he said.

I smiled again. 'I'd stopped talking altogether.'
'You?'
'Exactly.'
'Christ.'
'Yes.'
It was 13:17.

'I suppose her nurse's training helped,' he said.

I pursed my lips. 'She was a mother too.'

He rolled his eyes.

I explained that she'd had me go to the doctor. I did not explain the unusual nature of our discussion, mine and Mum's; how it differed from the skirted nature of our conversations, spoken, emailed, text; issues meandered around, shied from.

But yes, I told the man, my mother had spotted the tell-tale signs, namely the silence, and the way I sat at the kitchen table numb, incapable of 'sweating eyes'.

I went to the doctor, and was given a lengthy waiting list, plus tablets that came in a red blouse and yellow dress.

'Happy pills.'

'If you so say,' I said, said too I'd a long wait to see 'someone qualified', with too much time 'dwelling on it all', such that my mother, smart, desperate all the same, found me a purpose in the meantime.

'Taking care of Billy?' said Mr. Handley.

'Indeed,' I said. 'I'd to be up at eight-thirty. Gluten-free porridge ready for him by nine. It has a hell of a stench, sir, gluten-free porridge.'

Mr. Handley nodded. 'Did Billy recover?'

'Yes. Then no.'

'The kidney stones?'

'Pneumonia, that winter. A carer left a window open in his flat overnight. Billy hadn't the height to close it. Spared him

Murphy Who Talks

Hitler's bullets, less so the cold. So it goes.'

Mr. Handley nodded, said it was 'a pity', to which I said 'Yes', and he said 'I'd say he was grateful to you', and I said 'He was, he said so at the time, in his will also.'

'A nice inheritance?'

'Fifteen grand.'

'To Billy,' said Mr. Handley, lifting his pint, and I nodded, in lieu of having my own.

Mr. Handley took a sip.

'Murphy, it makes a nice change to hear you talk some sense. But what in blazes does this have to do with me going to another pub?'

I smiled, looked out onto the Seven Sisters Road like I was looking at Plečnik's castle, Charles's bridge, some unknown person's beer garden where I spent so many hours.

'Prague. With Billy's money, I started a new life in the beautiful city of Prague.'

Mr. Handley grimaced, then sighed.

'Couldn't you have just said that at the beginning? I got money from an uncle. Moved town.'

'I could. But I see you're after finishing your pint. Another for the road?'

Mr. Handley grumbled, yet accepted the 'offer' all the same, affording me time to tell him how I bought a one-way ticket, a room in a flat, a place on a teaching course, and a new life on the *other* side of the grass.

It was 13:24.

I told him of Prague, how I lived there four years, teaching English, doing this and that, that and this, sometimes up, sometimes down, getting on with the getting on of things just the way I would have done *here*, only with better architecture, and beer besides.

'I taught it all, Mr. Handley. Idioms, tenses, you name it, I taught it.'

'Reading, writing, listening and–'

'Speaking?'

I winked. 'An advanced course; my speciality.'

He scowled.

'Shut up, Murphy.'

He took a large swig of what was now his fourth pint of the day.

'Enough. I'm glad you enjoyed Czechoslovakia,' he began. 'Bu–'

'Czech Republic.'

'What?'

'Czech Republic. Czechoslovakia hasn't existed since 1993.'

Rules are rules.

Mr. Handley scowled, growled and folded his paper. 'Whatever. What's that got to do with me going to another pub?'

'Everything, Mr. Handley,' I said, though I don't think he'd have stayed to listen had I not offered him a free refill of his half-full pint.

'Why?' he asked.

'You can go down the road, all you like, Mr. Handley, but like I did *there*, you've to live in your own skin still, that's all I'll say.'

'Is it really?'

'What?'

'Is that all you'll say?'

'No, of course not.'

'Get on with it.'

'Brilliant, so.'

It was 13:26.

*

Murphy Who Talks

It was 13:27.

He was bristling, but still sat on his stool.

'Ah, I loved it there, Mr. Handley,' I said. 'The beer, the food, the newness of it all. But I brought myself with me, if you catch my drift.'

'Not in the least.'

'I still had to work. Pay taxes. Contend with myself. *Be.*'

It was 13:31, and once more, Mr. Handley scoffed.

'Murphy, you're telling me you came into some cash, moved country, and realised it wasn't all it was cracked up to be. So? I could have told you life's not all it's cracked up to be.'

I smiled. 'It wasn't the going there I came to regret. It was the coming back.'

'Why's that?' he said. 'Because *you lot* lost?'

I smiled again.

'No, Mr. Handley, not that. Because I fell in love.'

'With a Czech girl?'

'Yes.'

'Name?'

'Karolina.'

He smiled the smile of fantasy.

I told him about the red hair, the green eyes, the copy of *Na západní frontě klid* under her arm the day we met, when she sat at my table without invite, and asked me the pronunciation and lettering of my name.

'Murphy.'

'Like the beer?' she asked.

I was nervous, so I garbled 'Actually, it's a stout.'

We fell in love.

'What happened?' said Mr. Handley.

'She's a mother now,' I said. 'The kid is not my son. Let's just say at a certain point I thought the grass was greener here, in England.'

Sometimes it's better to Tippex history, than to speak it aloud.

The ageing man finished his pint; put his *Express* in his plastic Tesco bag and began to put on his coat.

'Well, Murphy, that was quite the story.'

'Thank you.'

'Nice of your Uncle Billy to give you fifteen grand.'

'It was.'

'And your Mum to get you up and about when you weren't *on top form.*'

'Indeed.'

He picked up his stick.

'You're still going to the Orang-utan's Bazaar, aren't you?' I said.

'I am, yes. I've every right to use my phone.'

And off he went, to the grass, greener or not, on the other side.

I scanned the pub. It was busier than it had been in months. The idea that we might save it raised notions of inner peace, themselves threatened by a boost in customer numbers. A topsy-turvy state of affairs. Things were on the up. The summer was afoot, the World Cup too. I'd had little time for the yoga but hoped to find some between the hours I worked, the football, and my friends, Donnelly and Con Connelly, who of late I'd neglected to see.

Naturally, it would end in disaster.

But oh, what fun we had in between.

Murphy Who Talks

Chapter Seven – May

(Two Months Before)

- *Murphy dicks about on his phone*
- *Ireland has a referendum*
- *Murphy loses the best part of a morning to social media*

It was 12:59 and it was the twenty-sixth of May and it was both cold out and warm out.

One moment you could smell the pavement in the air as the heat rose to your nostrils, the next you were gazing up at fluffy grey clouds that looked like if they didn't break soon you were in for a shower.

It was the day of the Champions League final in Ukraine, an English team against a Spanish team, sponsored by Visa, Heineken and Gazprom; the nations of the world united in competitive sport and scrolling advertising hoardings.

I would drink Amstel tonight. Advertising had no hold on me.

We'd the *right* kind of crisps now in the pub, and a Polaroid camera with which we took pictures of punters clinking glasses, reading books and, most important of all, talking *to* each other in London's increasingly trendy, busy and mobile-free pub, where mobiles were not banned but could not be used either.

I did not want them talking to me, but to see them talk to one another was another matter altogether.

I was enjoying the distraction, and basked in the glory of a busy bar, where people drank and talked, ate decent crisps and food, or read books. My mind was soothed by idle chatter or the sweet sound of a turned page.

It'd been like this now for weeks, and it was good.

But today was May 26th. I'd booked the day off work and, for the first time in months, I was optimistic.

Summer was around the corner. The Island still didn't know if it was coming or going but there was sunny weather to be enjoyed and, in the midst of it, a World Cup in Russia.

It was 14:02.

I'd sneezed. I'd had bacon with my eggs without worrying I'd the cancer, cooked the bacon without concern as to how the fat would make me fat and the bacon give me the cancer in good time. It was a special day.

I was of no mind to concern myself with the complexities of the world. I'd run, eaten, and was on my bed thinking what to do next, flicking through the social media I'd an addiction to, messages from friends and my mother, the liberal media and the football news too.

Will you be watching the game? read Mum's note, my reply *but if course*, amended to *but if course*, amended one more time so it read *but of course* with the addition of *fuck that word*.

Language, son.
Sorry Mammy, I replied
Enjoy the festivities, she wrote.
Oh I will, I replied, wishing her a lovely day besides.
It was 14:03.

*

Murphy Who Talks

I was meeting my friend Con Connolly at 15:00. I picked up my phone, the home screen a collage of hopes, needs, interests, vices and lofty ambitions; the Down Dog app I'd downloaded so I could practise yoga at home, the green owl of Duolingo, the Spanish lingo not learned in nigh-on two months; Tinder, Hinge and Happn, where I hoped to find love, or at least approval, and other things I wasn't willing to admit – even to myself – besides.

I read BBC News and The Guardian to know the world through the prism through which I knew it already, downloaded a podcast to tune out of it, and scoured Ryanair to fantasise about jumping about parts of it. I looked at the books on my shelf, flirted with picking one, but went back to swiping, scanning and skim-reading.

I read less than before and didn't write at all. The world didn't care for words. They'd always been the first and final act, action just the muddled fuzz in between. I felt their loss keenly.

It wasn't all bad. The apps helped me pass the time, scrolling, pressing, watching, gazing, which I did now, passing half an hour before heading off to meet Con Connelly.

It was 14:05.

I checked Instagram. Stephen had had a go at doing social media for The Purser's Retainer in order to promote its mobile-free USP, but had written:

Want to watch the big game without the missus bored on her phone all night? Come down to The Purser's Retainer, London's first and only mobile-free pub. #football #UFC #UCL

God almighty, we were in danger of going viral, and not in a good way. I got on the blower sharpish and told him to take it down. He did. I told him UFC was about cage fighting too, and he was relieved to discover why he'd been followed by an assortment of heavily tattooed, muscle-clad men.

I was proud to see him making an effort.

Onwards, I checked the Instagram; saw a picture of my sister with her children and my brother with his cat, and various friends going about the weekend in various humdrum and exciting and sunny and not so sunny ways.

It was 14:06, and it seemed everyone was having a lovely time.

I looked at Facebook without consequence and then Twitter, which overloaded me with fact and opinion, opinion and fact, the feed reflective of me, interests at once narrow and broad, though today two matters stood out, mainly:

>#Repealthe8th
>>but also
>
>#LFC
>
>and

#Together4Yes and #TogetherForYes, which read as if it were aimed at language pedants like my mother.

#scientists4yes sat above #RoadToKiev, and there was plenty #YNWA, of course.

For the layperson, that's 'You'll Never Walk Alone', which is what Liverpool fans sing, and Celtic fans too, and Borussia Dortmund fans for reasons I don't know.

I scrolled up and down for ten minutes, jealously.

As I watched a Dublin crowd hug, cheer and wave flags – some with three colours, others more – a childish FOMO coursed through me. *Here* in the bedroom, with the last morsels of the eaten bacon and eggs, I wished to be *there*; amidst it all, inside it all.

My primary feelings that morning, as I read about Ireland's abortion referendum? Pride? Relief? About fucking time? All of those things, yes, but let us be honest a moment.

Murphy Who Talks

My primary feeling was jealousy.
I was lonely. And in being lonely, I felt left out.

I closed the feeds, checked for word from Con, read an exchange from Mum.

Mrs. Burke's after telling me off in Peggie's for recommending Nenagh Castle to a group of tourists.
And?
Apparently, that's North Tipperary.
And Cashel is South.
Yes.
You should have known better.
Women don't have counties, Murphy.
You've been reading those Sally Rooney novels again, haven't you?
I have, yes.
Brilliant stuff.

She thanked me for sending the book in the post, I bade yet another encrypted farewell, put my phone away, and went to meet Con Connolly.

It was 14:11.

Chapter Eight

- *Murphy meets old pals Donnelly and Con Connelly in Erin's Rejoinder*
- *Murphy undergoes a character assassination at the hands of Donnelly*
- *Donnelly gives Murphy a lecture about dating apps, despite his lack of interest in them*
- *Murphy gets a text message of great importance*

Con Connolly was a carpenter, and I had known him since I was eleven. He'd two sisters (younger) and an older brother named Sean. His parents were from Kilburn, his parents' parents from Cork, West Meath, Kerry and Arbroath.

Growing up, he'd worn the jersey of and supported whichever national team was doing the best at any given time: Scotland in '98, Ireland in '02, England thereafter, speaking volumes of Scottish football, Con's unromantic practicality, and the commercial gold-mine that is a multi-cultural family (of sorts) to football shirt manufacturers.

I'd not seen Con since February. Most of his work was London-based, but for the previous few months he'd been up working on a project in Colchester.

Daisy, his ex-girlfriend, had split up with him the previous

Murphy Who Talks

summer, ending a six-year relationship he'd not the ability to admit had run its course, and so we were there now, the both of us, in Tufnell Park, muddling through, getting by, making the halfiest of half-hearted attempts to saddle up, move on, *try* again.

Con had recently moved to the area, having never lived 'in town', as it were, and was renting with strangers for the first time.

It was 14:57.

He was in Erin's Rejoinder when I arrived. Its innards were dark though not dingy, the bar oaky and long, a huge pool baize in one corner, a jukebox nearby, and several tables and rows of worn and weathered patterned seating dotted about the place. There was a faint smell of smoke, a hint of metal in the air off the fruit machine and steel counter poles. As I walked in, Con had his eyes glued to his phone, elbows popped out towards the doorway, and a Popeye rictus of concentration on his face.

He had a shock of sandy blonde hair and, like myself, looked shorter than he was, hunched over, lacking the schooling to sit – let alone stand – with confidence and purpose.

I walked over to the table.

'Another?' I said.

He lifted his eyes from the phone screen and nodded. 'Murphinho. Please.'

I pointed to his glass, with its thimble of still-there liquid. 'Amstel.'

He nodded. I walked to the bar and said, 'Pint of Heineken and Amstel, please'.

The Heineken was for me.

'Any scandal, Murphy?' he asked, as I placed the pints down, the one with the foamiest head my side.

'This and that,' I said. 'That and this.'
'Eh?'
'I've been busy. Work.'
He laughed.
'No, really.'
Con frowned.
'At The Purser's? The pub?'
'Yeah.'
'I thought you said it was dead.'
'Dead busy,' I said.
He said 'Oh?' and I leant in to explain.

I told him about the pub, the crisps, the mouse that had died though in fairness that was a bit of a pointless aside and he noted it.

'Murphy, what does a dead mouse have to do with any of this?'

'Nothing,' I said. 'Only it still haunts me to this day.'

'Go on, Murphy.'

So I did.

I told him about Stephen's wariness towards my plans and Mr. Handley's defiance, and the fact that he had discovered the grass was not greener on the other side, and by early April had decided to follow our rules, in our pub.

'You've banned phones?' he said.

I shook my head.

'Not at all,' I said. 'Only the use of them.'

Con sipped his pint.

'That doesn't make any sense.' He paused, looked at me, put two and two together and said, 'Actually, Murph, knowing you, it does.'

'Good man.'

'What are you up to?'

'Good things.'

Murphy Who Talks

And I explained.

'Take you, Con Connelly; Englishman, Irishman and Scot all in one.'

'Joker.'

'If you were to come to my pub, you'd not be allowed to touch your phone.'

'No?'

'No, we've a safe where you've to put it.'

'A safe?'

'For safekeeping. People like their phones.'

'Right. So people *aren't* allowed to use their phones?'

'No.'

'It's a ban then.'

'No.'

'How?'

I explained. 'There's nothing to say you can't bring your phone into the bar. It's only you've to have it on silent, and you can't do a thing with your hands. It's a matter of self-control, which is beyond most people, hence the safe.'

'I'm confused. Sounds like six of one, half a doz–'

I clicked my fingers.

'You know I've no head for maths, Con,' I said. 'Let's just say you walked in, and the phone fell out of your pocket and onto the floor.'

'Right.'

'And in doing so, the buttons smooshed, and the phone answered itself.'

'Uh huh.'

'Then, in that case, *yes*, you'd be allowed to take your call. You just can't be the active ingredient, as it were.'

'I see.'

'So it's no ban at all. Only you've to restrain yourself.'

Con nodded. Sipped his pint. Looked over my shoulder

then into my eye.

'Murphy?'

'Yes, Con?'

'You are one weird cat. It's nice to see you.'

I clinked his glass.

'Meow. And yourself.'

It was 15:03.

I asked after his work, to which he said 'Work's work', and I asked after his family, and he told me they were well, and for a while we talked about that and this and this and that until his phone buzzed, an irritating distraction.

He looked down, then up, and exhaled.

'Christ.'

'What about him?' I asked.

'It's Donnelly,' said Con.

'Christ.'

'He's joining us after all.'

'God help us,'

It was 15:05.

Loving Con was easy. Donnelly? Let's just say I loved him too.

He was a difficult man. Donnelly liked to talk, to argue, dismiss, postulate, denounce, pour scorn, and give out. He liked to be right.

He worked in sales. I accepted him, he was forever needling, critiquing and trying to change me. Somehow, it worked. Familiarity, I'd say.

It was 15:42. Donnelly had got an Uber here, and I had made the mistake of saying they were 'not my thing'.

'Why?' he asked.

I admitted that I found the company's business practices unethical. It was met with scorn, laughter and rolled eyes.

Murphy Who Talks

'If you're not earning, Murphy, you're not yearning,' he said.

'Righty-oh.'

'It's a dog-eat-dog world.'

'Do dogs actually eat other dogs?'

I looked at Con.

'No idea.'

'In this day and age, it's luddite to hate Uber,' said Don.

'Bud light?' I enquired.

'Shut up, Murphy.'

I winked at Con, who winked at me, laughed, and said 'You're a hypocrite too', to which I asked, 'How so?'

'I've paid for your Ubers plenty of times.'

This much was true. I was wholeheartedly opposed to Uber and its contractor-model business practices; opposed, that was, until the business end of a night on the town.

'You've got me there, Con,' I said, to which Donnelly cut in with 'It's a competitive market,' refusing to let it go.

I said 'I guess', to which he added, 'Their platform is user-friendly. They blow the competition out of the water with their service,' to which I said 'Price?' and he said, 'Yes, that too' and I hoped he might leave it at that, but of course, he'd to have the last word.

'Your thinking is backwards, Murphy.'

'Ass backwards,' I said.

'Yes.'

'Yes.'

'Good.'

'Brilliant.'

It was 15:44.

I didn't much mind being called a fool, eejit or 'utter weapon' by Donnelly. It was more habit than conflict, the lay of the land for most of our lives. I'd be lying if I said I enjoyed his company when he was at his worst, lying more still if I said I didn't draw some comfort from it. Foolishly, after checking the team news for the match ahead, I had left my phone on the table, and it lit up now, apps I'd not used in a long while still there on the home screen.

'Any kindling, Murphy?' said Donnelly, looking at the Tinder, neglected there, wedged between Spotify, Instagram and the Gmail.

'Nope.'

'Can we see your profile?' he said.

It was less painful to give in. I slid the mobile to him and yearned for the phone-free environment of The Purser's Retainer, where I could manipulate the ebb and flow of conversation, namely with Stephen, or Mr. Handley.

But here, a beep, lit-up screen or vibration led us into the unfamiliar. Contrary to what I'd told Con – for my own amusement – we *did* have a mobile-phone ban, thanks to the article published by my former employers.

Leave a Message

Can smartphone addict Marcus Hartley survive an afternoon inside London's first mobile phone free pub?

An eight-page spread, they'd twisted my idea beyond repair, a glossy feature butchering a complex idea into a simplistic message.

People came in droves.

The Independent did a story on it, the *Mail* too, one ripping off the other. *The Sun* and *The Guardian* got wind, and a group of influencers came, only to realise they'd no way to document their experience. We let them take selfies from over the road.

Murphy Who Talks

Two were mugged. One dropped his phone in a drain.

People were joyous at the novelty of it all, or they griped and moaned and ultimately gave in, to move on with their lives (Mr. Handley).

Now, faced with Donnelly's inquisition, I missed the Stasi-like control I had in the pub. At The Purser's Retainer we lived a fantasy, an idyll; no intrusions. Here, the same could not be said.

Donnelly was sat there, now, looking through my Tinder profile, less than amused.

'Murphy, you've got to show off,' he said, after a minute or so. 'That's how Tinder works. You have to present the *best* version of yourself.'

A car that'd squeezed through reddening traffic lights beeped, coming to a necessarily sudden pause.

'Like a PowerPoint?' I asked, to which he sighed, said 'No,' and 'Girls can tell if you're holding back'.

I nodded. Wondered when they were women and when they were girls. I looked at a 327a bus as it passed by the window, Josh Brolin glaring down at me from a *Deadpool 2* poster.

'Maybe I should promote my volunteer work.'

'Volunteer work?' said Donnelly, with a smile. 'That's great. Women love that shit. *Where?*'

I smiled. God if he was not a fool.

'Durex factory. Product testing. Purely pro boner.'

Unlike condoms, the joke was recyclable.

Con laughed. Donnelly shook his head. Told me 'Girls don't like dick jokes,' before looking at my pictures.

'The photos,' he said. 'These all have to go.'

'What's wrong with them?'

He pointed at one.

'You have a straw up each nostril.'

'It's fun.'

And another.

'You're making finger pistols.'

'It's edgy.'

And another.

'You look miserable.'

'It's sultry.'

And the last one.

'That's just a picture of your passport. You're *English*, Murphy.'

'It's tongue-in-cheek,' I said. 'Brexit, eligible bachelor, freedom of travel and all that.'

'It's a desperate attempt to show you're Irish,' he said. 'And you *know* it.'

Himself Josh Brolin, and Ryan Reynolds in the costume, floated away.

'I know,' I said, my ability to withstand his scrutiny punctured. I whisked my phone back. 'It was only a joke.'

I told myself I didn't care what he thought about where I was from, nor what I thought about where anyone thought I was from, including myself. It didn't matter. Nations were bullshit. Cultures inherently demarcated by exclusivity over inclusion.

My claims were bullshit too. Of course, I cared. Whatever my conscious motivations at the time, I had undoubtedly wanted women to know, if not that I was Irish, that I was not fully from here, England. That I was something other.

Not just another anonymous white man in Holloway surfing the web from a position of lonely fortune.

Unique.

'Who wants a pint?' said Con, reading the room well.

'Yes, please,' said I, Donnelly too.

It was 15:54.

Murphy Who Talks

Donnelly liked dating, so he went on many dates.

Connelly did not, but nor did he like being single for the first time since the age of twenty-five either, so he was giving it a try. And then there was me, who did not like it at all. Why? Who knows? I was shy, averse to rejection, and had found that tongue-twisting, paragraph-long answers to simple questions tended to put – ward? – women off.

Long and short, I'd come to the conclusion that online dating wasn't for me. Donnelly thought me mad. Online dating was what people did now.

And as much as myself and Con had been content to talk about this and that, that and this, Donnelly's attention was fixed upon an app that five years earlier he'd have dismissed as the stuff of weirdos and creeps.

How quickly things change.

He was there now, busy swiping right but mostly left, detailing what was wrong with the various women he saw online.

'Pub lunches, brunches and hungover Bloody Marys.'

'What about them?'

'Who doesn't like those things?'

'Jehovah's Witnesses?'

'It's uninspired,' he said, swiping left. 'This one, she wants a man who's "ambitious".'

'And?'

'That means money.'

'How do you know?'

Donnelly smirked. 'Come on, Murphy.'

'Right-oh,' I said, not really knowing.

Donnelly swiped left again, thankfully now using his own phone.

'She seems nice,' I said. 'Likes fitness, Netflix and travel.'

'Mmmm.'

Con handed me my pint.

'Thank you,' I said. 'What's wrong, Donnelly?'

'Look at this bucket list. Alaska, Machu Picchu, New Zealand. The Galapagos Islands.'

'A bigger carbon footprint than Shell.'

This wasn't Donnelly's concern; his that she was like everyone else, the apps having a tendency to show we'd much in common with one another, which was undesirable, staid. He swiped left and quickly left again.

'What was wrong wi–'

'Don't go there,' said Donnelly. 'We all have our preferences.'

I smiled at Con.

'Oooh, hello,' said Donnelly, looking at a Swedish woman in gym gear, with red hair. It was like the angels had aligned his mother's hopes and his desires. He swiped left.

'What was wrong with her?

'One eye slightly above the other.'

'You're going grey.'

Donnelly glared at me.

'Swipe away, Donnelly.'

I sipped my pint, Connelly sat with his phone, doing whatever it is he did on it, and Donnelly swiped left mostly, right occasionally, and made a point of swiping left on the ones who stipulated *No hook ups* while appreciating the woman who'd written *If you're just looking for a ride, get a bike*.

'Ha,' is what he said.

Well, with the pair of them there, on their phones, the three of us talking but not really talking to or with one another, who was I to do any differently? There was a message, on the WhatsApp, for me.

It was great fun

Donnelly ranted on, about the importance of 'profile curation', about how girls picked up signals based on 'worth', 'value' and 'differentials', such that I didn't know if he was trying to have me coupled up or traded for shares in Exxon Mobil.

A clack of pool cue against white, then white on red or yellow or maybe even black, and I pined for The Purser's Retainer.

I slipped my phone back into my pocket, and listened to Donnelly drone on about that and this, this and that, smiling inside after something that'd happened two days back, an event that I will recount

right now.

It was 16:04.

Chapter Nine

- *Murphy meets Rebecca West*
- *Naughty hands*
- *Of frogs and flexibility*
- *Sex-Face yoga*
- *Dates*

The yoga studio was busy. I worked long hours Thursdays, from four 'til midnight, sometimes longer, now that we'd an afternoon crowd, an evening crowd, any crowd at all.

Business was building if not yet booming, my back roaring for all the kegs I'd to shift around the cellar floor. My back was taut, the pain in my lumbar had returned, so I'd decided to go back to yoga, even if it meant paying through the nose now that the introductory offer had lapsed.

'Morning,' said the receptionist as I walked in. 'Do you have your card?'

She had red hair, thin lips, and green eyes, and looked like Jessica Chastain. Or Bryce Dallas.

'Yes,' I said, beeping it on the scanner, sitting down.

The thermometer on the wall read thirty-eight degrees. I could hear tinny music coming from the studio as the previous

Murphy Who Talks

class came to an end and students meditated briefly, and I looked around at all the people in the hallway; fat and thin, Lycra-clad, some in shorts, a few with their own mats. They were all trying in their own way, for their own reasons. Some were beautiful, others, like myself, would soon be a glistening mass of fat and sweat, and we'd to try and put the thought out of our minds as we focussed on the yoga.

I breathed in, hoping the heat would loosen the tightness in me after shifting kegs. Suddenly, I felt a strange warmth on my knee. I looked down.

It was a hand. Its owner, the woman sat to my left, turned, realising what she had done.

'Jesus! said the voice.

'Christ! said mine.

'Sorry!

'Don't worry! I replied.

The two women stood by the studio door had a nice little giggle at the loudness of all that.

The woman retracted her hand.

'Sorry about that,' she said.

It was, I realised, the blonde lady I'd seen some months ago, at my first class. She was wearing multi-coloured Lycra and had a leather bracelet around her right hand.

'I thought you were the bench,' she said.

I shook my head. 'No, I'm Murphy. The bench is there.'

I pointed at the bench. She smiled.

'Thank you. Is that Mr. Murphy, or First name Middle Name Murphy?'

'Neither. Just Murphy.'

'Just Murphy?'

'Aye.'

She nodded her head, apparently, though I've no idea why they say that in books. What else do you nod, after all?

'I see,' she said. 'I'm Rebecca. Hope you like saunas.'

She clapped her hands. What else could she have clapped?

'Right everyone, let's get physical.'

A herd of Lycra, Nike and other synthetics walked as one into the hot, sweaty Bikram class and Rebecca turned to me.

'I'm your teacher, Murphy. Are you coming to class?'

I was.

There were over thirty students in the room. Class began with a sharp intake of breath, knuckles under the chin, elbows raised to the skies, eyes too on the exhale, those same elbows brought together, a loud collective gasp emanating around the room, as if news had spread that Whole Foods was going under.

'Raise your arms, interlace your fingers, make sure your toes and heels are touching,' Rebecca said. 'Now, bend your body right and left, left and right.'

We moved like metronomes, 'til she said 'When you're even on each side, stand up straight. Gaze towards the mirror, keep the weight in your heels and bend to the right,' a movement we repeated on the left.

'Feel a nice stretch there. And go beyond your flexibility.'

We paused in the middle, reached upwards, bent backwards.

'Look towards the back wall,' said Rebecca, though I could only go as far as the ceiling. 'Take a short break as you come back up, then bend over slowly, and wrap your hands round your ankles.'

I pulled hard when she said to and lost my balance.

Throughout the class, Rebecca walked around, her skin glistening from sweat even though she wasn't doing the poses herself. She'd a frog tattooed on her right foot, a Sanskrit tattoo on the nape of her neck, **पुरज्ञ**, and I was curious as to their meanings.

She glided about the place, gently encouraging bodies into form, massaging taut and tired limbs.

'Gently Murphy,' said Rebecca, as I tried to touch the floor with my hands. She pressed her own against my back. I jolted.

'We have a skittish one,' she said aloud to the class, and subsequent sniggers, her soft fingers like a warm flannel to an electric fence, the long-forgotten touch of human skin a novelty to me. I relaxed, through a mixture of embarrassment and shock.

'Don't worry. If you can't touch the floor, grab the sides of your legs.'

I did, calves tight as wire, and was told I'd 'get there in the end' by someone I imagined was there to begin with.

'Namaste,' said Rebecca, at the end of the class, to which the others said 'Namaste' back while I lay on the floor, soaked, exhausted, lying there like a baby.

After a minute or so in the dark, hot room, I picked up my mat, wiped up a pool of sweat from the floor with my towel and left, saying goodbye to the receptionist.

Sitting outside a moment, enjoying the cool evening air, I heard a voice.

'Murphy.'

I looked up. It was Rebecca, smiling, maybe pityingly. She was now wearing a white sports fleece, zipped up, and she sat down beside me.

'Did you enjoy the class?'

'Absolutely,' I said. 'Hard as you like, but I liked it all the same.'

'What?'

'It was enjoyable.'

'Really?'
'No, but it's good for me. I'll be back again, I'd say.'
'You need to,' she said.
'Why so?'
'You're stiff as a post.'
'Ah.'
'And you make a sex face when you stretch.'
'Oh?'

Rebecca scrunched her eyes, flared her nostrils, pursed her lips, vibrated the lot in unison, and began to laugh.

'Like that,' she said, as a couple of students left, waving goodbye. 'Don't worry. It gets easier over time.'

A train hurtled by in the distance, to Kings Cross or Finsbury Park.

'The yoga? Or the sex face?'

Cars beeped their horns on the Holloway Road.

'Both, I would imagine.'

Bashful, I averted my gaze, noticing once again the tattoo on her foot, with its red lips and cartoon-like eyes.

'It's not Pepe the Frog,' said Rebecca.
'The racist cartoon thing?'
'Yes. I've been told it's uncanny.'
'Well, there's a pass—'
'It's in honour of a pal who died.'
'Ah.'
'The irony is he was called Toady.'

I paused, wondering what I should say. I wondered if it would help to speak of my own loss, but reconsidered at the thought she would think I was playing grief blackjack.

'If you squint, it kind of looks like Kermit.'

She laughed.

'Your squinting face is a lot like your yoga face.'
'You should see my sex face,' I said.

Murphy Who Talks

There was a pause. Awkward, so. Another train passed. Rebecca asked me if I myself had any 'terrible tattoos.'

'Two,' I said, showing her the ones on my arm and chest, of which I shall not tell you. Why?

'Both awful,' said Rebecca.

That's why.

She nodded, said 'I'm not one to talk,' and showed me the **प्रज्ञ** on the nape of her neck. *Wisdom*.

She had, she told me, quit her job in marketing at twenty-four, and moved to Thailand to train as a yoga instructor.

There, she'd fallen for an older teacher with a thing for symbolism, Sanskrit and younger women, had been persuaded to get a tattoo by way of 'living in the moment' and 'with utter freedom', before later discovering he had lived freely, on several weekly and borderline scheduled moments, with her hitherto best yogi friend, Jessica.

'Sometimes it's better to be none the wiser,' was all I could say.

'I think that's quite long in Sanskrit,' she replied.

Another train rumbled by.

'People can be mean.'

'People can be bastards, Murphy.'

'That's not very zen.'

'I'm no longer at work.'

The lights must have just gone from one-bulb red to one-bulb green, as there were various beeping sounds up on the Holloway Road.

'Fair enough. They can.'

Even now, looking back, I swear to Christ, I was about to do it myself; ask her out, take a risk in life, for a change.

Perhaps because I didn't, I can insist that I did, there, have my lips parted, to say words that filled me with a fear greater than Christmas Mass, sex education and a WhatsApp message from Juliette combined, words that even the distance afforded by the apps rarely afforded me.

Do you want to get a drink sometime?

The world was going to pot, but The Purser's was on the up. Racism normalised, argumentation idealised, patriotism valorised, populism promoted, lauded and in a fiscal sense, highly patronised. What did I have to lose?

'Fancy a quick drink?

I couldn't believe my ears. 'Yes,' I said.

I would have asked her myself, had it gone on any longer. Honestly.

Chapter Ten

- *Murphy enjoys having a secret*
- *Watches the football*
- *Assesses his obsession with Ireland and his childish petulance too*

So I had a secret. I'd gone for a drink with Rebecca, at a bar in Islington, had a lovely time, and said not a word of it to Donnelly or Con, who I was with, now, in a bar just off Church Street, with kick-off approaching.

I was in the gents when the message came through.

I found you!

What?

Your Hinge profile was her message, *Jesus wept* mine.

Rebecca had asked to see my profile, only for me to refuse, yet she had found it now, with the same pictures that, of course, Donnelly had only earlier today critiqued.

I see you've advertised your Irish passport on Hinge she wrote, now, on the WhatsApp.

A sweetener in the event of a No Deal. A little joke. It's really not that important to me, I replied, to which Rebecca wrote *I think you lie*, which was of course true.

Identity was a matter of convenience, to latch onto or

discard at will, a compensation for the fact I could walk streets with ease, into jobs with likelihood, expectation too.

Way back when, it was words where I'd found my identity, but I'd left them now and they me. Ireland would have to do, an identity I could hide or flaunt as I saw fit. I was the default, anonymous, fortuned face of a white supremacy, whether I liked it or not; Paddy with a London accent, whitey and his synthetic woes, for whom identity was less a matter of misfortune or insistence, more a way not to feel small.

Rebecca saw it, Donnelly knew.

During the evening, she had asked me if I was 'into football', to which I'd said 'Yes', and she asked if I was looking forward to the World Cup, to which I said 'Very yes', and asked then if I wanted Ireland or England to win and I told her Ireland hadn't quite made it this year.

'That's a pity,' said Rebecca.

'A crying shame,' I said. 'They nearly qualified, only to be thumped in a play-off against the Danes.'

'Those troublesome Danes.'

'Indeed.'

A sucking sound, as she sucked on her orange drink; an Aperol Spritz.

'Will you support England instead then?'

'I will.'

'Because you're English?'

'No, because it would be churlish not to.'

'And because you were born here?'

'Just as Boris is an American.'

'And grew up here.'

'So did the King of Bahrain.'

'Really?'

'Harrow. The school. Not the place.'

Murphy Who Talks

A sip of my pint, like I was hiding away.

'Face it, Murphy, you're as English as Churchill.'

'The dog off the telly?'

'No.'

I shook my head, said I didn't see it, England and me, said of course I was a little English, though not a lot, said that I didn't see an England I wanted in on 'til 'England wants the Jamaicans it's had shipped and returned to sender', 'til 'England acknowledges the Jewish Prime Minister it had', the 'Nigeria it made', the 'Indian from India plundered and Paddy who paved its roads and gave it its corn', then no, I'd no interest in England or being *of* it, but I did concede there was a 'bit of me' that looked forward to that day.

Rebecca sucked the last of her Aperol Spritz drink and widened her eyes.

'Quite the rant, there, Murphy,' she said.

This was our first date.

'Sorry,' I said.

'Another?' she asked.

'Yes, please.'

'Heineken again?'

I said 'Yes please' to that too.

It was 20:06.

'Lads, will I get us some crisps? I said.

'Yeah, good shout,' said Con. Donnelly nodded.

They only had Jackson's. I put my principles to one side. The game began.

There was a Senegalese man – he'd a yellow, green and red wristband on his left arm – watching the game, sat alone on a padded stool, a Liverpool shirt on top and powder blue, faux-ripped jeans below. Him aside, it was just us and two barmen. The pub up the road had been crowded, and I had wanted to go in, only for Donnelly to overrule it. He worked with people, spent hours convincing them to buy advertising space, charmed them. But he only liked strangers on the phone, via email, in an expensive bar in central London. On his clock, he'd time only for me and Con, and a few other lads from school, his family too, for the most part. In a way, it was an honour.

Now that we were in a quiet bar, away from the din, I fantasised about what it would be like to be in the midst of it, the noise and life of the pub up the road, just as I'd looked at the Twitter feeds from the referendum, and the fans travelling to Kiev for the game, and wanted to be in on that too.

A petulant desire to be included in a society that had always afforded me a place.

Liverpool lost the game.

Occasionally, Rebecca still messages me to say how she's overcome the silence of her room with Spotify, Netflix, the noisy electric heater from the attic, despite the perfectly working radiator in her room.

I'll tell her the lengths I've taken to refine the pleasant silence of my life; namely the Bose headphones that work best with music, less so podcasts that never fully drown out clatter or a human voice.

Then and there, though, the evening of the Champions League final, I wanted to let in all the noise; the hopeful crowds on Twitter, the men in the pub discussing the game, the messages she sent on the WhatsApp that I read in the toilets, and in furtive glances, fearful as I was of interrogation from Donnelly, Con besides.

Pranayama
You looked that one up, she wrote.
Savasanna, I replied.

Murphy Who Talks

But not that one.
How do you know? I wrote.
You spelled it wrong.
Ah.
Try another one. Harder.
Dandayamana-Bibhaktapada-Janushirasana
Did you use Google, Murphy?
I did, yeah.
You're no fun. No fun at all.

I asked her if she was having a nice evening. She told me she was. She had gone out for drinks with fellow yogis, in Angel, was *knee-deep in Sancerre* and *kale talk*, she said, and between the one and the other was *having a lovely time.*

Brilliant stuff, was the last I'd wrote, and knew from the two-tick blue the last she'd read.

It was still light out, summer starting to make itself seen and heard not in the height or brightness or intensity of the sun but in its opposite, the gently slinking orangeness of the streets of Stokey, which were bathed in the afterglow of a day that'd been overcast in the morning, sunny the afternoon, resplendent the evening, now a hazy sort of in between.

It was 21:53.

'Another?' I said, pointing first to Donnelly and then Con's glass. Both nodded.

When I came back, Donnelly was looking down at Con's phone.

'Any scandal?' he said, as a notification unblackened the now bright iPhone. The man could smell a notification.

Con lifted the phone and took a look.

'Match?' asked Donnelly.

Con said 'Yes', Donnelly 'Let's have a look.'

With resignation, Con passed it over.

'She's fit,' said Don, Con 'Yes' and when shown I answered honestly, and Con seemed pleased.

'You don't seem too happy about it,' said Donnelly, as I asked him 'Whatever happened to the teacher?' he'd been seeing a few weeks before.

'We met up once,' said Con, and Don asked had it ended morning or night.

Con answered honestly, and when asked if he'd be seeing her again, answered honestly to that too.

A Liverpool player on the telly looked sad.

It was dark out now, May in defiant reminder of spring's early-to-rise, early-to-bed mentality, summer's diligent, quietly retiring cousin. There'd been a clamour of excitement outside the bar in Stokey due to a burst drain that at first had me thinking the heavens had opened, a gaggle of folks stood around inspecting it. Donnelly lambasted the Liverpool goalkeeper, who had made a mistake, while we sat on the bus. Con watched a video on his phone.

'He's steamrollered him,' said Con, as we rode back to Holloway, me watching the highlights, and scrolling up and down on feeds where:

#LFC and #Repealthe8th and #TogetherForYes sat beside #Together4Yes and #RoadToKiev even though that was now done and dusted.

I liked and liked as I watched videos of rainbow-coloured flags and flags with liver birds and turned to the boys to make a suggestion.

'Another at The Mother Red Cap?'

Con nodded, Donnelly said 'Yes', and the three of us got off the bus and walked up the Holloway Road. The match had been anticlimactic, but as we walked into The Mother Red Cap, there was a message on my phone.

Murphy Who Talks

It was odd; phones, suddenly, didn't seem so bad.

Sorry Kermit, the message read. *I'm on the mojitos. See you at class tomorrow ;)*

'What you doing?' said Donnelly, as I lagged behind.

I looked up. 'Oh, nothing, I said. 'Just texting my brother.'

Donnelly nodded, his suspicious grin and glint gone.

'Right. Ok.'

I held the door open for him.

'After you,' I said.

The three of us went inside.

Chapter Eleven

- *Murphy tries to take on the local branch of the IRA, with disco and with dance*
- *Murphy gets punched in the face*
- *Cleans the shelves behind the bar*

I walked into work on Monday morning, an albino panda, skin the colour of chalk, eyes dark as coal. I did not make it to yoga the morning after the Champion's League final.

Sunday is a day of rest, I had said, to which she'd replied *tsk, murphy, just tsk.*

Hadn't the grace to capitalise my name.

All the same, I was in a good mood, as when I said *I might pop in for a class tomorrow* she replied *you need the practice ;)*

'Blimey. What happened to you?' said Stephen as I walked in, seeing the two black eyes I'd picked up at The Mother Red Cap late on Saturday night.

'I ran into a little trouble after the Liverpool game.'

'You mean you got into a fight?'

'Absolutely not, Stephen,' I said, affably as I could. 'Fight suggests a competitive element. There was nothing of the like. I wouldn't be into that sort of thing. I'm a man of peace.'

'What happened, Murphy?' he asked, and I'd to tell him

Murphy Who Talks

how I was set upon by a group of boys.

There was a jukebox, two banks of cushioned, patterned, storied and chewing-gum matted seating, a barman with elbows knobbly as Con's and hair the colour of plaice, and a group of young men guarding the pool table with their lives, Irish rebel songs blaring from the jukebox about killing men from the country where they were born if not fully from, much like myself.

I told Stephen that the lads began singing along with 'gusto' and 'mindless fervour' after myself, Don and Con Connelly had settled in for a few pints in a far corner, to get away from the situation, more amused than bothered, ourselves guilty of the same crime in years gone by perhaps.

'And then?' said Stephen.

'And then the punching happened.'

'And how did that happen?'

I couldn't recall every detail, I said, but mentioned the fact Con had riled the young men up by sashaying his arms from side to side, grinning ear to ear, engaging in a sort-of mocking, traditional Hiberno dance to the tune of 'The Fields of Athenry'.

'Why were you in The Mother Red Cap?' Stephen asked, knowing as he did the good and bad of every pub in the area.

I've to admit now it was a fair question and come the morning seemed rhetorical, but when I thought on it deeper and later, I knew exactly why.

'We had yet to have our fill.'

A raised eyebrow off him, an empathic one all the same.

So I went on to tell him about the six lads playing pool, Plastics like us, English like us, in between like us; drunken, slunken huddled over pints boys like us with differences woven through; a Celtic cross on one lad's arm, Bhoy's jersey on another's form, the fiddly-dee fiddly-die songs coming off the jukebox machine that we'd a mind to think silly now in our intelligence, the added digits in our age, who knows?

'What?'

'They were semi-Irish lads singing very-Irish songs,' I said. 'Making fools of themselves.'

'I see.'

We'd stopped in, I told Stephen, to see the night through, yet to be sated by our day on the tiles.

'You were having a skinful?'

'Quite. A catch up, if you will.'

'With?'

'My friend Con, who I'd not seen in months, and my friend Donnelly.'

'When did you last see him?'

'January. He'd a holiday and then an office-swap with a colleague in Singapore.'

'Bully for him.'

'Indeed.'

I told Stephen that though we'd been out all day and now night I still felt lucid at the time, maybe because I was watching the little Fenian Londoners as the red and yellow balls bounced against and into pockets, while they added IRA bits into the song, as Con grinned, mocked and sashayed his arms.

I'll be there with bells on, I'd written to Rebecca, though was yet to hear back, and sat sipping, silently, as Donnelly and Con talked, and the latter sometimes mocked the lads on the pool table.

I sipped and looked at my phone, a digital acolyte once again, looking, waiting to hear from her, hoping, passing the time, scrolling up and down on the feed that said Vote4Yes and repealthe8th and HomeToVote and YNWA.

*

Murphy Who Talks

'So how did this skinful turn sour?' said Stephen.

I explained. Explained how I had gotten up at a certain point, maybe bothered, with childish, male impatience, having not heard again from herself on the mojitos. I fed a couple of pounds into the jukebox machine, I told Stephen, so the rebel tunes gave way to 'I'm in the Mood for Dancing', much to the young men's disdain.

The barman with the plaice-coloured hair giggled, as did I, Con and, to his credit, Donnelly too. But the six boys round the pool table took exception, the Nolan Sisters Irish like rebel songs but, to their minds, not quite Irish in the right way.

Stephen shook his head.

'Are you saying they punched you in the face because you played a disco tune from the seventies?'

'No,' I said, as it was not strictly true. 'They didn't start swinging until 'Lady in Red'.'

'Murphy?'

'Yes?'

'You're a fool.'

'An eejit. A goon.'

Stephen shook his head and walked to the coffee machine to make himself a drink.

I put the drip trays into place, wiped the oaken bar. It had hurt; the punches swung by the young, angry men. But I didn't regret it. For the first time I could remember, I'd stood up, in my own way, for what I thought to be right.

If we were to chase after our Celticness, we'd to accept it all, good and bad.

The espresso vessel roared.

There was no point playing tunes by long-dead men on the day Ireland had voted to make full humans of women, no point to banging on about Trevelyan's corn or men of internment as brown people rotted in direct provision and wire-garlanded cells.

The milk steamer whistled.

No point to glorify Kilishandra only to ignore that it's easier to win the Lotto in Ireland than it is to buy or even rent. If we were to play giddy and free with 'I Useta Lover', we'd to admit the Ireland we grew up visiting had only ever existed in our shamrock-tinted minds, and if we were going to be Plastics with any honesty, credibility, identity or sense of a *place* at all, we'd to accept that Ireland had moved beyond us, was better for it, and that Chris de Burgh was no less Irish than Patrick Pearse nor Boyzone nor John MacBride.

Ours, a nation of many colours, so often distilled into one, or at best three.

The cup graced the saucer with its presence.

'Sorry, Murphy,' said Stephen. 'I didn't catch a word of that, what were you saying?'

I sighed. 'Nothing, just a little ramble.'

'Right,' he said, looking out of the window. 'If anyone asks, say you were mugged.'

'By who?'

He shrugged. 'By a gang.'

'Which one? Bunty Hovan's Rangers? The Splenetic Seven? The Jovial Thirty-Two?'

He left me to it.

It was Monday, it was quiet, and I'd time to clean the front and back of the bar.

It was 12:16.

Mr. Handley was in now, and a few others, drawn by the novelty of the phone ban, the numbers of which – I'd noted – had started to dwindle.

The eyes were sore, memories of Saturday vague yet returning, bits and pieces via WhatsApp as Con asked *how* I was

Murphy Who Talks

doing and Donnelly did too, surprising me with a *hope they're ok*, to which I responded *I'm fine*, having initially typed *grand*.

The dishwasher gurgled.

Mr. Handley rustled one page of his paper over another. I took the glasses off the shelves and fed them one by one into the dishwasher, and felt good to be getting on with the getting on of things.

The shelf was sticky with beer and blackcurrant and so I cursed whoever had drunk Guinness and black but thanked them for the opportunity as I worked at it with a J cloth.

I kept feeding the glasses in and out of the washer, thinking as I did how I'd taken the piss out of the young fellas, how all the same I'd not been able to say, simply, 'Boys, would you ever pick another song?'

Afraid to take them on openly, I'd opted for the *runaround*, through the medium of dance, and gotten two black eyes for my troubles.

Stephen returned, saw my work, and said 'Nice job, Murphy', to which, I have to admit, I felt a pride. He asked me to empty the blue recycling bin beneath the till, so I went out back, and separated the various recyclables and the non-recyclables.

I returned to find two customers looking at the menu, which I'd had reprinted in Cyrillic, for fun.

'Mate, what's going on here?'

'Cyrillic Mash, sir,' I said. 'A new menu we're trialling.'

'But I can't read any of it.'

'That's half the fun.'

'But I can't eat gluten,' said the first customer, and 'I don't eat meat' the other.

'I'd avoid numbers one through six,' I said, to veggie lad, and 'Stay away from four, six and ten' the other.

'But I can't read it,' said the first lad, to which I said 'Boys, for goodness' sake now, they're written numerically', which was true.

I had explained what they had to avoid, only not what they could have and what it would be.

'What the hell is this?' said the one lad.

'A journey into the unknown,' I replied.

'Eh?'

The other lad.

'An adventure. A risk. A *surprise.*'

'This is absurd,' said the other, and the pair of them walked out, or tried to, though they had to return and demand I open the safe so they could retrieve their phones.

They were no fun, no fun at all.

When they were gone, Stephen returned from the office. I was done with it. Identity, words, lark and debate.

It was time for the next phase.

'Stephen, I said.

My manager turned from inspecting the Cyrillic menu he hadn't known about 'til moments earlier.

'It's time.'

'For what?'

'For the sound of silence.'

A car, a Citroen Biryani, whistled by outside.

'Murphy?'

'Yes, Stephen?'

'Shut up, Murphy.'

I smiled. I had him in the palm of my hand.

Little did I know that my plan would run into conflict; with a World Cup in Russia that promised much, and Rebecca West, who I've to admit never promised anything at all.

Murphy Who Talks

Chapter Twelve

- *Murphy tires of the customer*
- *Bribes Mr. Handley, yet again*
- *Shhhhhh!*

The Purser's Retainer was getting by.

The beautiful, hip young things had come in droves and then stopped doing so at breakneck speed. It was a popular fad, but like all fads, had worn off so, while I'd freed my workplace from one of the things that bothered me – the phones, with their distractions, noise, feeds and irritants – I'd yet to find the necessary balance between profitable custom and inner peace, and the CPO was still hanging over us.

We were still getting decent crowds, at least compared to before the changes.

Word of mouth had melded into word of print, and for all its many flaws the media had served us well; it had written about us, the novelty of a phone-free pub at such odds with the way of the world that they were willing to ignore our own flaws; the dodgy seats in the men's jacks, the one missing in the ladies' too.

The novelty had worn off for the early adopters, who'd adjusted, grown bored and I, the very same.

But as with Shoreditch, Theatreland and the Millennium Eye, weekenders from outside London who'd read about us in *Time Out* still poked their heads around the door.

We'd gone mainstream. I didn't like it, only a bit of me did.

So, this was what it was like to be at the centre of it all.

According to Stephen, we remained in the red, however. We sold pints. We shifted a decent amount of wine. The Taytos sold like hotcakes.

Chef was busy in the kitchen, the new menu, an appropriated mix of Cajun and Irish influences (the Po' Boy Colcannon was a smash), going down a storm.

But we'd still overheads to pay; the leccy bill for the ice machine, the fans, the bar lights, the back lights, the front lights at night, the lights that lit up the beer taps. And of course, there was all the noise.

Do you have Jacksons crisps?

I just need to send one text, can I get my phone back?

Guys, guys, guys. Let's put a tenner in the jukebox and only play songs with 'phone' in the title. It'll be hilarious.

The customers, they drove me mad.

Had I ulterior motives with what came next? Not at all. We'd to keep our fingers on the pulse; to grow with and shape trends, to be one step ahead. The phone ban had helped, but it was a temporary solution. People couldn't live without their phones. But maybe they could live without words.

I was determined to find out.

The Grayling project was taking shape; glistening like a Big Mac, juicy and seductive from afar, questionable up close.

I did not want to lose my pub.

The estate beside the Grayling was crumbling and old, the land a goldmine given its proximity to Finsbury Park station, the people who lived in it less so. It wasn't just about me. Yes,

Murphy Who Talks

I wanted to watch the World Cup in peace and yes, I wanted to minimise my interaction with other people, but there was a community to be saved. There was only one thing to do.

Stephen was sitting at the bar, playing Buckaroo with Mr. Handley. I let them finish their game. It was only fair.

That sort of carry-on wasn't long for the pub.

'A ban on speaking?' he said. 'When you said you wanted to turn The Purser's Retainer into a silent pub, I thought you only meant people turning off their phones.'

'I did. At the time.'

'I thought you were only exaggerating with the words idea.'

'I was not.'

'He's finally gone doolally,' said Mr. Handley.

'I have not.'

'He's lost it.'

I looked at him. He glared at me. I put a hat on a donkey, which bucked its Roo.

'God damn, you, Murphy.'

Two customers talked about house prices, at the table by the window.

'Murphy,' said Stephen. 'This is a pub. Banning people from talking to one another will be the end of us.'

'No, it'll be a new beginning,' I said, said too that we were facing 'diminishing returns,' that we couldn't be short-termist, and that if we were really going to stop the pub from closing and ward off the CPO we'd to 'double down' on the 'silent element' of our London Pub.

'Go on, Murphy,' he said, much to my surprise.

He was nursing a Coca-Cola. His plaid shirt was crisp and well ironed, his hair, what there was of it, trimmed and groomed. The man had a new lease of life, it was clear, and I wanted it extended and broadened.

I explained to him that we'd to shake things up, think of

something 'bold' but also 'fresh' and 'new', and so mooted the notion of a silent pub, where noise was discouraged, speaking prohibited.

Yes, I admitted, this time, it was to be an outright ban, with a speaking jar for customer fines.

Stephen was dubious. In fact, he called me an 'eejit', and, much as I was trying to leave all *that* behind, I couldn't help feeling a bit of pride at having gotten under his skin so. And yet, to my surprise, with a glint in his eye and a rubbing hand on the goatee he'd curated on his chin, Stephen came around, or was on the verge of it. I just needed to seal the deal.

I told him how 'mad times' called for 'mad ideas', explained counterculture, anti-advertising, and inverse conservatism, how going against the grain was the best way to go with the grain altogether, whilst turning a profit.

'Sure,' I said. 'At one time the pub was a pub and a pint a pint, a bar stool a bar stool, a floor or floor. But those days have gone.'

'Wrap it up, Murphy.'

'We're living in times when the rules have been turned upside down.'

I walked out from the serving side of the bar, could hear the unmistakable cry of a Land Rover Try-Hard in the distance.

'Men have always sought escape from the noise of life, Stephen. But now they want to mute the sound. People are tired, they don't want community, community's dead.'

'Is it?'

'Look over the road.'

He did, and in fairness to him, he agreed.

'They just want to be left alone. To think and read and write in peace. To *be*.'

'Didn't you used to be a writer?' said Stephen, with some accusation.

Murphy Who Talks

I told him 'No', and began telling him of Todd from Perth, a lad I'd once known, though Stephen waved it away angrily.

'Murphy,' he said. 'It's beginning to sound like you simply don't want to talk to people.'

I looked at Mr. Handley, and the two customers in the window seats.

'The very opposite, sir,' I said. 'Talking to people's my butter as much as it is my bread. I could stand here and talk to you all day.'

'I believe that.'

'Good,' I said. 'But this is about survival. It's not about me.'

'Right,' said Stephen. 'And how will banning conversation in the pub lead to success?'

I sat on a stool.

'People are tired of three things. Brexit. Experts. And talk. We're powerless to do a thing about the one and in no danger of being the other. But talk, all the damn *talk*, now that's a thing we can do something about.'

A Fiat Clueless beeped at a Volkswagen Uruk-hai.

'Trust me, Stephen. When the world's doing one thing, do something else. It says football you say quiet; Joe Bloggs demands fish you give him chips. Left is right and right is wrong.'

He shook his head.

'You know what, I don't even like football. Get on with whatever it is you want to do, Murphy.'

And so it was. We became *London's First Silent Pub*.

They loved us for it.

I was not just a barman now. I was an entrepreneur, a businessman. The phone project had been a notion, an idea, the brainchild of a committed lackey, an eager member of staff, a man in need of distraction from the thoughts in his head, and the dull reality of an eight-hour daytime shift behind a bar.

To the question of what a pub could *be* I'd the answer; and the answer was to turn the noise down.

The CPO was going to be defeated.

I'd not seen Rebecca since the evening of our drink in Islington.

'I'm off to Aldeburgh for a bit,' she'd said, as we parted. She was off to see her mother, who lived alone, and was struggling with diabetes. 'I'll see you when I'm back.'

Whether she meant here, on civvy street, or there, in the yoga room, I wasn't sure.

I was a busy man, suddenly, and there were humans in my life, again; Don, Con, maybe Rebecca too.

But the noise ban remained a priority. Word needed to get out, before I'd the World Cup to contend with, and a bar filled with preening, screaming, flag-waving England fans.

Elsewhere, whales were dying, Peter Stringfellow too; migrants were drowning, and the President put tariffs on British steel, which Britain could do nothing about, needing him more than he them; a Donnelly to their Murphy.

But on my own patch I'd a pub to save, so I paid a local homeless lad two Betties and a pack of Benson's to put up posters around the Seven Sisters Area, all of which had the same black background and white lettering to the fore. It said:

Shhhhhh!

@

The Purser's Retainer

Coming Soon

It was 14:53.

I didn't want to get ahead of myself. It was only a drink.

But this is a novel, in which powerless anger can be wicked and active rage, the diminished can be something, the

Murphy Who Talks

powerful weak, the ugly beautiful, the unhappy happy, the hopeless hopeful, the voiceless voiced, the English Irish, the Nigerian British, the unequal equal, the entitled stripped, the sex-starved happy and sated, the inflexible flexible, the clown all that he was, nothing less and nothing more; sad and joyous altogether in one package.

We had kept in touch, Rebecca oddly receptive to the bizarre things I said.

What do you reckon they call kiwi fruit in New Zealand? I asked.

Erm, kiwi fruit?

But wouldn't they just call it fruit the way the Danes call Danish bacon bacon and the Chinese Chinese Whispers only whispers?

Good question, she replied. *I'm not sure you're meant to say chinese whispers these days.*

No?

No.

Ah.

As for the bacon or the kiwi fruit, Murphy, she wrote, *I've no idea. But it sounds like you're having a quiet day at the office. How come you're using your phone?*

We're done with that, I wrote, to which she replied *I thought that was your 'USP'* to which I wrote *It was, but we're moving forward with another idea*, to which Rebecca wrote *Oh?*

We're going to ban talking.

Before the one-tick grey had gone two-tick grey she'd come back with *Ban talking? That's madness.*

That's what they said about putting a man on the moon.

Is it?

Probably.

I see. Well, enjoy. Sounds like an awful idea. And I won't be visiting.

I looked up. Stephen had walked into the pub, with a sullen

expression on his face.

'Right, Murphy, I did what you asked.'

I'd requested that he write the following on the chalkboard outside the pub:

As of June 6ᵗʰ The Purser's Retainer will be a conversation-free environment. No shouting, no speaking, no chatting, no bell-ringing, phone-calling* or talking of any kind.

*but you will be allowed to use your phones again. On silent.

The Management

The ban was afoot, silence awaited. And Rebecca would not come to visit.

Why? I wrote.

Because I absolutely hate silence.

'You look a little flushed there, Murphy,' said Stephen. 'Do you want to go for a cigarette break?'

I answered honestly.

Now, I sit in my room, looking out at the snow, a whole metre of it piled up on the ground outside.

The thought occurs that perhaps I did it purposely all along, each scheme and plan. She had, I recall now, told me on that first night that she didn't like silence, albeit in a roundabout way; had told me that she liked life and noise and dancing, less because of music or movement or the sex or electricity of it, more to counter voids; the empty silent bedroom, the voice in the head when faced only with the deadening sound of silence between the four lonely walls of an empty kitchen.

She did tell me, so maybe I did it to keep her at arm's length, scared as I was of losing her from the outset.

All I know is that once I'd got Stephen on side, and had him write on the chalkboard, and seen the St. George festooned state of the pubs from *here* to *there* between the Seven Sisters and Holloway Roads, there was no turning back.

I contacted Glen. He couldn't run another feature, but put me in touch with Edward, a colleague on another magazine.

This is right up our street Murphy!!!

They sent a photographer and a writer. The interview took place outside the pub, to hammer home the point that we respected the rules as much as we made them.

There was a photo of me shushing the camera, another of Mr. Handley reading the magazine. I'd had to bribe him with a whole day's Pride so he'd not read *The Express*.

To his credit, Stephen had finally cottoned on, realising the offset of ten (Mr. Handley really went to town) pints of Pride was nothing compared to the exposure.

The punters came in droves.

They videoed the bar, they drank their pints, they took note of the passing cars, the roaring and unseen madmen, the electric saws, the hammers and drills, and when they wrote *Are you showing the World Cup here?* on the pieces of paper next to the beer taps, I wrote back *Absolutely*.

They read books and magazines. They smiled at one another but didn't say a word. Some walked in without seeing the huge cardboard cutout of myself outside (from the magazine) with its shushing image and 'No Talking Inside' instruction.

'Come off it, mate,' said one man, when I told him of the ban, with a finger to my lips. 'You having a laugh?'

'Absolutely not, sir, I'm a man of business,' I said, in a

hushed whisper. 'A gatekeeper of tranquillity, a protector of peace.'

I was whispering fierce quiet. He had to lean in.

'Why are we whispering?'

He whispered himself now, to give him his due.

'There's no talking in this bar.'

'Why?'

'It's a silent bar.'

'What the fuck's a silent bar?'

'I don't want to have to patronise you, sir, but–'

'Just give me a beer.'

I pointed to the clipboard on the bar, where I'd printed menus with the beers labelled 1-10, motioned with a pen, so he would choose – in silence – his favoured beer.

'A Heineken for fu–'

I pointed. I glared. I put my finger to my lips and awaited a collision between my face and his fist, yet all the same pointed warningly towards the Silent Jar, which was gathering dust, had only a ten-pence piece from Day One, when Mr. Handley had said 'This is a lot of fucking rot' and waltzed out, only to return half an hour later.

The punch never came. The man looked at the menu, then me, then the menu again.

With the pencil, he put an X in 4.

A pint of Amstel. He was happy out.

It was a roaring success. The punters came, most stayed. They drank more in silence than the mobile-phone deprived hipsters of before. They drank, they studied, they lingered and read.

They were, I noticed, mostly men. Thoughtful men? Reflective men? Unhappy men desperate to drown away their sorrows? It didn't matter. They were paying men.

As for me? Was I at peace?

Murphy Who Talks

With five questions in the above two paragraphs, it would appear unlikely.

The bar was silent. I'd quiet; no interruptions, no complaints, no moaning, no Mr. Handley telling me what he thought of the Romanian bakery down the road and the likelihood they were flouting the same health and safety regulations he was adamant had been forced upon us.

A silent bar gave me time to think. And I thought. About rent prices. About the poor people over the road and the rich ones soon to be their neighbours. About the poverty on the Lorraine Estate, which I saw each day in the people that came and went to flats the same size and sometimes smaller than mine, with more people in tow, children usually. I was glad to have silenced the world outside of me, but in doing so had forgotten about that constantly ruminating one within.

The football would be on soon. I could watch it in peace and occupy my mind. Unbeknownst to me, however, something would happen to me the following morning that would change the way my mind, body and soul operated altogether, and that is a thing that I will recount right now.

Chapter Thirteen - June

(1 month before)

- *Murphy's success at The Purser's Retainer makes him bold*
- *Murphy falls over, gets back up again*
- *All Murphy's hopes and dreams come true*

It was Saturday, 9:03. I had the whole day off.

The previous evening, Mr 'Bros before Hoes' Donnelly had cancelled a drink last minute, and I'd read *Autumn*, by Knausgaard or Smith, you can decide, and I'd sent Rebecca a text to say I'd be at yoga in the morning *bright eyed and bushy tailed*, adding shortly after *was wondering if you fancied a drink Saturday? I have the evening off*.

Not hearing back, I went to her class all the same. You've to be bullish with these things. Unprecedented success in my working life had taught me that.

The sun was out but with sleep in its eyes, hung orange and glowy in mid-air, the bastard threat of late-season hay fever in my nostrils. The Holloway Road was quiet, other than a road sweeper cleaning the kerb: an Evian bottle, a McDonald's milkshake cup, a Coke can, a Quavers packet that floated above the pavement. It was globalisation in litter, and I was on my way to Bikram clad in Nike trainers, an Adidas sports top,

Murphy Who Talks

and Under Armour shorts from the Sports Direct up the road; a sweatshop owner's wet dream.

I went to class.

It was 9:32.

As a pale and distending pear, I sunk towards the floor. Left leg over right knee, hands in prayer, I marvelled at the parallels between yoga and my erstwhile Catholic faith and will say this for Christianity: You've to bow, beg, pray and kneel, but never on tippy toes. The same cannot be said of Bikram yoga.

Rebecca was at the front, concentrating on her work, the class, the students, myself included, doing her job, I told myself, suppressing the wanton, childish, male need inside me, to be spoken to, seen, heard and considered.

'Stare straight ahead, stretch your arms in front of you. Keep your back straight and, if you can, try to balance on your toes.'

The sea of fluorescent, Lycra-clad acolytes did as instructed, myself included, 'til the tippy toes element, at which point I slipped and fell, landing on one knee.

Rebecca smiled.

'Try again, Murphy. Just do the first two parts.'

I did as she said, outstretching my arms, straightening my back, staring ahead. The electric fans gushed; the heat of the room made worse by the heat outside, already in the thirties. Bodies yelped; their owners' breaths filling the room. The receptionist out front was telling a student Yin Yoga began at eleven, and Rebecca told us to do round two of the pose, walking over to the door at the side of the room, opening it as she did.

'No point in us dying for Bikram,' she said, as a gust of cooling air rushed in and gasps of gratitude – from us – out.

It was only the third of twenty six movements, and I was

tired, sweating, hot and resigned, but at the thirteenth we'd a respite as we lay on the floor for three minutes, doing nothing, catching our breath, and the cool air, which Rebecca let in from the air conditioned reception rather than the stifling street outside.

'Relax here a few moments,' she said. 'Ankles touching, hands at your side. Stay sane.

A few light chuckles, a shook head off the woman next to me, not a fan of Rebecca's humour. A Fiat Cluedo rolled along on the street outside.

I gazed at ceiling tiles, wondering if I was seeing things through sweat-blurred eyes, as a figure began to hover over me, mouthing words.

Drink more water? Go in peace? Chim chiminey cher-oo?

She leant down, picked up the water bottle beside me.

'Take a drink of water, Murphy,' she said. 'You're overdoing it.'

I nodded. She leant closer.

'I'm free from seven.'

I nodded again.

'Wind-removing pose,' said Rebecca to all and sundry, clapping as she rose, and the students lifted their knees to their chins.

It was June.

It was roasting hot out. The World Cup was around the corner. I had somehow become an entrepreneurial barman, and despite all the bickering, criticism, bother and chatter, it seemed as if the summer was filled with the promise of hope, amidst the litter and the noise. The country didn't know if it was coming or going, the fans were still pumping out hot electric air, the streets paved with dust not gold.

I still sneezed in the mornings and checked my tissues,

worried I'd the cancer. Still worried about my purchasing choices, whether importing a family of five too-cheap bananas from *there* to *here* was okay, about the Nike trainers on my feet and the Sports Direct shorts my hips, and what that said of the decency, if any, within me. I still tiptoed around the flat so not to disturb Juliette, despite her lack of repeated complaint, and I had found that while banning mobile phones had made us popular, and trendy, it had served only to block out their influence inside the pub. Outside, it all returned; anxiety, fear, worry for the world at large, if only to distract myself from that within; family and friends, CPO and pub.

Breathing out, I wondered if Bikram was doing me any good and, breathing in again, concluded that as I'd a date that night, in a way it was.

That was good.

As I lay with my ankles facing the window and walls, breathing into the hot air, I was free of worry a moment. And then I remembered that before meeting Rebecca, I'd to endure Donnelly's charitable attempt to get me 'back in the saddle.'

Namaste.

I could smell the protein in the vending machines and muscle-clad arms of the men and women all around me. I'd been to gyms before, but it was the first time in a while I'd set foot in those futuristic, pin-code-locked tubes standing between me (£24.99 p/m and willpower aside) and good physical shape.

Donnelly didn't know it, but I'd been going to the gym for years. I liked to exercise alone, listening to podcasts without being shouted at by people fitter or more competitive than me. I lifted, pushed, pulled, ran, and kept in shape, more or less, without telling a soul.

As I didn't talk about it, or document it in Instagram form, Donnelly had no idea. It was not that he was inherently vain, more that he bought into things when the things were the norm, and now that it was normal to post videos of yourself working out in the gym, that was what he did. It worked for him.

Once in a blue moon, Donnelly tried to do something generous, and in fairness to him, when Donnelly thought he was being helpful, he really did think he was being helpful. I was meeting Rebecca in the evening, and had not told Donnelly, or Con for that matter, so it would not become filled with promise, hope, and ultimate failure. Sat between fantasy and reality, I wanted to keep it that way. Donnelly and Con were the real world, Rebecca the other. I was compelled to keep the two apart.

Donnelly, meanwhile, was determined to get me 'in shape' and 'back on the dating' scene, and shortly after my yoga class I'd gotten a text off him.

Sorry I had to cancel last night. Gym at 14:00?

I replied to tell him that I'd signed up yesterday and would see him there *with bells on*, though of course I'd a membership already.

I went and saw him there.

It wasn't just fitness Donnelly had in mind. He wanted to take photos for my dating profiles and, I suspected, his Instagram, he a self-proclaimed expert on all things love; an Aldi-brand Casanova, a no-frills Valentine, the everyman's Paddy McGuinness.

No, scratch that. Paddy McGuinness is the everyman's Paddy McGuinness.

If you asked Donnelly something, and it didn't interest him, you'd not hear back. But when it did, he was there in a heartbeat, such that I suspected he spent as much time glued to his phone as I did mine. Now, he was in a helping mood, the confused, maladjusted, oddly better part of him having walked into town.

Over the years, this iteration of Donnelly had turned up at pivotal junctures, reminding me – us both – why we endured our friendship.

In Year 9, when Gerard Thomas unwittingly insulted my late father, Donnelly punched him without me even having – or wanting – to ask. In Prague, it had proved impossible to get hold of Donnelly via the Facebook or email, yet when I moved back, unwell, on medication and heartbroken, he had found time to sit in pubs and drink with me, our reason for being there masked 'neath phrases; 'a few jars', 'an excuse to drink on a Tuesday'.

And when I was made redundant, Donnelly found time to do the midweek quizzes he so detested (they shone a light on his lack of interest in music, TV, film and geography) and go for pints on a Monday after he'd been filming in the gym.

Yes, on a day-to-day level, Donnelly was useless. But he appeared in times of crises; a man of extreme, all or nothing, random acts of decency.

Sometimes, in more cynical moments when I thought ill of him, I thought Donnelly projective. But there were times, crucially, when he was digitally and physically present, distracting me from my problems, talking when I wanted to, or not, allowing me to sip and watch and escape.

At times, he got it right, simply listening, or offering blunt truths.

'This must be fucking a cunt for you.'

'You thought about going back to therapy?'

'If you fancy a change of scene you can stay at mine a few days.'

But my woes were timestamped, however. A gestalt.

If I alluded to ongoing pain, or the day-to-day loneliness

that had followed me throughout my time on this earth, he tended not to respond, at least not until I myself moved the topic away, texting words like *Few jars on Saturday?* or *Who have you transferred in this week?*

The pair of us colluding, he to segue from discomfort, me my disappointment with him.

As a man, you couldn't just say you were lonely. You had to have a reason to be sad.

But just lonely? That was a crime, a flaw. A little pathetic.

It is what it was, it was what it is.

Either way, I was now considered in need of his decency. It had been a long time since my return to England, and I had been through ups and downs and, importantly to his mind, off the all-important dating scene too long.

We were in the PureGym near Finsbury Park, a stone's throw from the Purser's and the gleaming, growing Grayling Estate.

It was 14:06 and it was June and it was hot as hell already, and we were there under the fans, the pair of us dressed in synthetics, me lifting a kettle bell as he took photos.

'Why's it called a kettle bell?' I asked, to which he said, 'Murphy, don't talk, it's bad for the photos.'

'Oh.'

He chattered his teeth. 'You'll look like you're at the dentist.'

'I see.'

'You just keep squatting.'

'Right oh.'

Donnelly continued to take photos, snap, snap, snapping away as he circumnavigated me. We did this, and then he had me move onto a treadmill.

'Won't this look a little choreographed?' I asked, and he said 'Get with the times, Murphy.'

Murphy Who Talks

I asked if sweating on a treadmill was a good look.

'If you didn't sweat so much, we wouldn't have this issue.'

'I'm on a treadmill,' I said, to which he said, 'You're a sweaty man' and me 'You're right there.'

'Stop, talking, Murphy,' said Donnelly, so I did, snap snap, onto the next machine, Donnelly unsure which one we should go for. 'The elliptical machine?' I suggested.

He shook his head.

'Women use elliptical machines, Murphy. They're not impressed by them.'

'I see.'

'The rowing machine?'

'See elliptical.'

'Right.'

We settled on bicep curls. He snapped away. We went to the pub.

It was June, bastard warm out, sun fierce, beautiful.

It was 14:56.

'Could you take a photo for us?' Donnelly asked a passing customer, so we could tick that box; *photo with* one *male friend*.

They did. We drank our pints.

Donnelly asked about The Purser's Retainer, checking messages on his phone and, I suspected, uploading the video he'd had me film as he benched weights.

'A talking ban?'

'Not a word.'

'What happens if someone speaks?'

'They get a warning. Second offence is the Silent Jar, third is they've to leave.'

Donnelly nodded. 'It's not for me.'

A voiceless Sky News presenter on the telly above was mouthing some news good or bad in the world.

'Why so?'

He looked up from his phone.

'What kind of people go to pubs to sit in silence? Normal people go for a catch-up, a chat, a *natter*,' he said, imitating his mother's strong Leitrim accent.

I nodded.

He said we 'should hit the park' and get a 'few more photos' while it was still light.

I said 'Fine, let's go,' and in between thought as to which sorts of people went to pubs to sit in silence, and mumbled 'the rest of us' to myself, though if I'm being honest, I was unsure if it was not so much *us* these days as it was *them*, nor where I stood on the idea.

We went to take photos.

Murphy Who Talks

Chapter Fourteen

- *Murphy goes to a swanker-than-swank wine bar*
- *Rebecca drinks an orange drink*
- *Murphy has a lager drink*
- *Murphy solves awkwardness with crisps*
- *Things happen*

I didn't know it then, but I never had fallen out of love with words, only their misuse. Rebecca would unveil this to me, through bullshit aversion, stretching, and an acute talent for candour and directness.

It was 19:14.

We were meeting at The Olive Branch, a wine bar on the Holloway Road.

After seeing Donnelly, I'd gone home, read a while, and looked in the mirror, teeth of England, hair of Ireland, nerves of glass. Walking to the cupboard, I looked at my clothes; nine white shirts, two pairs of blue, denim jeans. A pair of brown shoes for fancy occasions, red New Balance trainers for summer, blue for winter. I went with red.

Like sneezing, WhatsApping and work, my clothes gave consistency to my life. As I was leaving, I bumped into Juliette.

'Murphy.'

'Juliette.'
'How are you?'
'I am well. How are you?'
'Fine. Where are you going?'
'To a bar.'
She laughed.
'You are always in a pub, Murphy.'
'Not a pub,' I said. 'A *bar*.'
Juliette frowned.
'What is the difference?'
From head to toe I ran my hands. 'Would you dress like this for a pub?'
'You look the same as you always do.'
'Really?'
Juliette paused a moment. 'You have taken a comb to your hair.'
'You're not wrong.'
'Are you wearing perfume?'
'Aftershave.'
'What is the difference between perfume and aftershave?'
'One's for women, the other men.'
'What?'
She had a point, so I tried to explain the hypocrisy of the distinction to her.
'Murphy?' she said, shortly after I had begun. 'I have no idea what you are saying. Enjoy your evening.'
'Thank you muchly,' I said, leaving as the sound of Juliette asking 'What is muchly?' rang in my ears.

We met outside The Olive Branch, had a peck, a cigarette, and went inside. The bar was busy, full of clinking glasses and a clientele filled with vim, confidence and self-esteem.
Aliens.

Murphy Who Talks

As well as visiting her mother, Rebecca had spent a weekend in Rome with her colleagues Irene and Sophie; 'good wine and full-fat ice cream at home' her summary as to which was the better of the two.

'It was nice,' she added of the Italian capital, as if out of necessity.

It was a busy Saturday night. England had played Nigeria in a friendly at Wembley. I'd seen swathes of fans in white and red, with red and white faces and flags going towards the train stations earlier. And I had seen swathes of young Nigerian men and women who I imagined were British like me, half-British like me, or not British at all, like me, depending on how you or they looked at it.

Rebecca had an orange drink, me yellow.

'I've never been to this place before,' I said.

'You picked it.'

'I know.'

'Why?'

'It seemed like a place where trendy people go.'

Rebecca sipped her orange drink.

'And you're not trendy? You're wearing New Balance shoes.'

Red was a smart choice. I thanked her.

'So,' said Rebecca. 'On a typical night, this wouldn't be your haunt?'

I sipped my pint. 'Not as such.'

'Where would you usually be found?'

'A crumbling Irish pub frequented by unemployed, old, or unemployed old men. Mostly dead.'

'Which?'

'Eh?'

'The pubs or the men?'

'Oh. The pubs. The men, some perhaps, most of them are getting by I'd say.'

'Good for them.'

We clinked our orange- and yellow-drink glasses.

It was 19:25.

I looked around The Olive Branch, with all its trappings of class and refinement. Cork bottles. Wine glasses hung upside down like cattle in an abattoir, tessellate-tiled walls, framed photos of orange groves in some Mediterranean locale, a photo of a silver fox with a fag and Ray Bans; expensive lights, which I'd to admit were at the right level, the music too; just a tinkle in the background.

Fair's fair, you've to give credit where it's due. Rules are rules.

'You don't look comfortable,' said Rebecca.

'I'm cool as a cucumber,' I said, looking around, hot as hell and nervous as you like. 'It's just this place reminds me of my old friend Billy Pickings.'

'Who?'

'He ran a pop-up burger and milkshake van that doubled up as a cocktail bar in New York.'

'Sounds fun,' said Rebecca. 'What was it called?'

'Shake n' Cattle, in a Roll.'

Rebecca put her orange drink down.

'Was that a joke, Murphy?'

I paused.

'Yes.'

I pointed to the picture of the cow on the wall, dragging a wooden cart. Rebecca turned, looked at it, laughed, and said 'Fair enough. Jokes are fun,' had another sip of orange drink, and looked me dead on. 'But why's it easier for you to look that cow in the eye than it is me?'

I answered honestly.

Murphy Who Talks

The look I got was one not of scorn, but pity.
It was 19:32.
I saw on the clock behind her head.

I always wondered what it was that made happy people drink Aperol Spritz. Something in the rhubarb, a lightness in you that made shelling out eight pounds for a bright orange drink seem okay.

We'd gotten to the nub of it, why I told tall tales (her words); made up people's names (Rebecca, again), me admitting that in saying that and this and this and that I got out of various situations to avoid *situations*, wheedled my way out of difficulty so not to face difficulty, conflict, discord.

Yes, I'd to admit, it'd worked for and against me these years, and I admitted to her too that it was difficult to look people in the eye as it left me vulnerable and when asked why I'd to say 'Fear, I suppose' to which Rebecca said 'Fear? There must be a bit more to it than that.'

I smiled.

'Tak jo, there always is.'

Rebecca frowned.

'What does *takyo* mean?' she said, to which I said 'That's life, c'est lavvy, that sort of thing' and she asked me where it came from. I had to admit that it was Czech.

'Where you used to live?'

'Yes.'

'With your ex-girlfriend?'

I'd to admit that too.

It was Rebecca's turn to smile.

'Do you make a habit of referring to exes on dates?'

I answered, quite honestly, that I didn't make a habit of going on dates.

'It shows.'

This was not unfair. Rebecca advised me to 'rein that sort of thing in a little' and I'd a joke that began with rein and ended in dear.

But it was better written than said, so I nodded, and said, quite simply, 'Noted'.

The pair of us had awkward sips of our orange and yellow drinks.

On the plus side, I don't even know if it was before or after 20:00.

It was 20:09.

Rebecca had gone to the bathroom, and I'd checked my phone.

Peter Gabriel came in my ears, lightly, off the bar's small, expensive speakers.

Rebecca returned, drank some of her orange drink, and the conversation shifted to work. Work had been hard lately, she said, the heat of the yoga studio compounded by the weather outside, her routine out of kilter having been away, her usual enthusiasm tested by the sheer discomfort of the stiflingly muggy June air.

She asked me about the pub, if anyone was 'into it', this 'silent bar thing.'

'Droves.'

'Really?'

'Plenty.'

'You're mad.'

'A raging cajun' danger man,' I said. 'A shifty loon. A cuckoo. I know you're no fan of silence, but you should check it out, Rebecca. You might be nicely surprised.'

She put down her orange drink.

'Silence isn't my friend,' she said, to which I asked 'Why?' and she said 'Gives me the shivers.'

Murphy Who Talks

It was my turn to tell her there had to be more to it than that. She smiled sadly.

'Of course.'

To daters, people and things are props, and so it was for us, as we veered from certain topics and towards others, safe in the knowledge that if all went well there were the certain topics to which we'd come back.

Rebecca noticed a young woman showing off a large, gleaming ring that'd likely cost a kid in the DRC an arm or a life, and the subject of engagements was therefore raised, Rebecca asking if I had ever been engaged.

'No, you?'

She had. Rob, from university, had proposed a couple of years after graduation; 'Dull, kind, reliable Rob', whom she had loved, then not loved, and broken with upon realising he was a mirror more of what she didn't want than a picture of what she did.

He was kind, decent and, fatally, yielding. He was not her father – whose influence on her view of silence would soon become clear – which had appealed, until it did not, at which point she broke off the engagement realising, as she did, that he'd become more bulwark than lover against the possibility of repeating her mother's unhappy marriage. It'd ended well, she said, 'til a little later, reports drifting back to her that Dull Rob now referred to her as 'that ungrateful bitch', taking the view as he did that he had *stayed* with her while she was on Erasmus in Madrid.

Stayed with her.

'Cute,' said Rebecca, of the notion, before having another sip of orange drink.

During her first two years in London, she'd worked in marketing, been promoted once, and left it behind after her relationship's end to hop, skip and jump to Thailand, where she trained for the yoga, which is what she did now, and was cheated on by a manipulative older man, which was not.

Her father had said going was a terrible idea, her mother called it risky, and between her disdain for the one and sympathy for the other, she knew she'd made the right call.

'Brilliant stuff,' I said.

'Quite.'

And so we'd discussed the lives of others and fragments of her own, and with two orange and two yellow drinks between us and topics flirted towards but not fully touched on having boomeranged, such that we'd to do the very thing that made me avoid looking people in the eye; communicate.

Rebecca told me that her father had worked in the City most of his adult life, was in his mid-fifties now with the liver of an eighty year old, and that her folks had divorced when she was nineteen due to his intractability, the 'request' submitted mother-side years earlier.

'The family that stays together obeys together,' she said, adding that a mix of 'medieval literature and Sauvignon Blanc' got her through the divorce, though given she was at Keele at the time, it may have 'been a given.'

After her parents' divorce, Rebecca's mother moved to a small flat bought with settlement money. Her father's offer of 'not a fucking penny' proved inadequate with the courts, who settled on a fair few pennies more, concluding that two children, a career foregone and years of keeping an unhappy home vaguely redolent of cohesion was work after all.

This is a novel. Dreams can come true.

Rebecca told me that her mother was from Kangaroo Island in Australia, as if it would be anywhere else.

'That's very far away,' I said. 'Are there lots of kangaroos?'

Murphy Who Talks

'There are,' said Rebecca. 'When the British arrived they found them to be very docile.'

'Why so?'

'They'd never seen humans before.'

'Did they become friends?'

'No,' said Rebecca. 'We ate them.'

So it goes.

She told me that while her mother had occasionally been wistful for the arid, large island of her youth, she now talked about it with such nostalgia that Rebecca was of a mind to think she was planning on going back, despite her health.

'She forgets herself,' said Rebecca, to which I said 'How so?' and she said 'There's a reason she left in the first place', which turned out to be a mixture of boredom, lack of opportunity and a desire 'not to be a farmer, housewife or both.'

'How did that go?'

'She studied in Adelaide,' said Rebecca, adding that she'd then moved to London, started to work, met Rebecca's father, got married and, in turn, become a housewife, albeit 'not on a farm.'

'Swings and roundabouts.'

Rebecca took a sip of her orange drink, looked pensive.

'Do you see her much?' I asked.

She nodded.

'Every four to five weeks,' she said, adding that she did so more these days, since her mother had been diagnosed with diabetes.

'I'm sorry,' I said.

'For what?'

'That your mother has diabetes.'

'Did you give it to her?'

'No.'

'Then don't say sorry, Murphy.'

'Sorry,' I said.

'What was that one for?'

'For saying the wrong thing.'

'There's no need to apologise.'

So not to act the parrot of myself, I took a sip of my yellow drink.

'Well done,' said Rebecca, as if reading my desire and mind.

'Thank you.'

'Do you find it hard not to say sorry?'

I nodded.

'How very English.'

Turns out I do have the odd spiteful look in me. Rebecca laughed. At, not with.

'What about you? Do you see Ma and Pa often?' she said, before looking a little regretful.

'No,' I said.

'Oh?'

'Ma moved back to Ireland,' I said, said too before she asked about it, 'Da died when I was young,' and she said 'Oh sorry.'

But she did not look surprised, and I would soon find out why.

It was shortly after the sorrowful valley of sorries, and some tentative questions about my own family, that Rebecca explained her disdain for silence, telling me as she did that it'd been the hallmark of an upbringing in a large house of embittered, needless and spiteful quiet.

In circumventing conversations about her father's own cruel quiet or loud spite or reckless spleen (the worst of it, she said, being you never knew which you were to get), her mother would play the radio in the car to avoid talk of this and that, 'Our family troubles' masked by 'Heart and Radio Four'.

'At least it wasn't Kiss, or Magic FM,' she added.

Murphy Who Talks

'Brilliant stuff,' I said, only so I'd say something other than sorry, sorry to hear that, I'm sorry your father was a shite, or some such shite.

Now, years later, Rebecca still felt the need to fill silence wherever it emerged, in talk and chatter, in radio and telly, in Spotify and whichever pirate radio station happened still to be on the frequency of her small digi alarm if she found herself awake in the late hours of the night.

A kettle boiled without making the tea.

A door opened on a cold day to let birdsong and the sound of people and cars in.

And of course, phone calls with friends, to 'catch up' if only to drown out.

There was a small silence then, for which I almost apologised, but had the wherewithal not to, wherewithal also to remember my grandmother's belief that all of life's woes could at least be met with, if not solved by, snacks.

'Will I get us some crisps?' I said.

'That would be fab.'

So I did.

They only had Kettle Chips, to be expected in such a place. Rebecca was delighted, ripping the bag open, diving into a world of parsnip and sweet potato.

She'd no idea what she was missing.

Respectively, me and Rebecca had another couple of yellow and orange drinks and then, for reasons I'll never know, I suggested cocktails, getting wrapped up in the atmosphere of the place. I went for an espresso martini, which she politely declined, saying 'Caffeine gives me the shits.'

She had an Old Fashioned instead.

Murphy, I thought you said you were working!? said the message I read while Rebecca was in the toilet, to which I replied *I was on a double, but now I'm not*, to which he'd time to write *so where are you?*, this all in the Three Amigos WhatsApp thread Donnelly had set up for the World Cup.

Rebecca returned, I hadn't time to reply. It felt good to leave him wondering.

It was 21:06.

A Subaru Specific beeped at a tardy Honda Taramasalata outside.

'So,' said Rebecca.

'What?'

'Earlier today, I came across an article you wrote.'

'I didn't know I was that good,' I said.

Rebecca closed her eyes in disgust.

'Murphy, that's gross.' A pause. A longer one. She spoke. 'You're allowed to apologise for that.'

'Sorry.'

'Forgiven.'

An Audi Misfortune arrogantly sped through the nearest set of lights as I said, 'How did you find my article?'

'I typed Murphy into Google.'

This is a novel.

I knew from the timbre and tone of her voice which article she was talking about but had hoped to high hell we'd talk about anything and everything else, so I said, 'Was it the one about gin distilling with Serbian artisans in Novy Sad?' to which she said 'No'.

'My exposé on Estonian saunas with the photographer Kenan Spillane?'

'No, Murphy.'

'My piece on the Charlie Chaplin Festival in the summer of 2016, when I lost my hat? Or the article I did on nettle picking in Le Havre?'

'No.'
'So, it was the one about my mental breakdown?'
'That's the one.'
'Oh.'
'Righty.'
'Oh.'
'Indeed.'

I should have known, and perhaps in truth I did within me, wanting her to find 'me' there on the Internet, wanting to hide, only wanting also to be seen and found out. In just the same way the country didn't know if it was coming or going, maybe I was just as bad, not knowing if I wanted to be seen, read and heard, or to seek safety and hide.

I'd left behind words and not written a jot in the best part of a year, but that didn't mean the words had left behind me. There's a thing called the Internet, and nothing goes away, not the dick pic you thought you'd deleted long ago, nor anything to do with AOL, much to everyone's surprise.

'I liked it,' she said. She screwed her nose, as if there was a bad smell. 'I'm not usually one for–'

A pause. 'Candid stuff. It was good though.'

'The money was too,' I said, recounting the piece; my fall, the period spent at home, the gradual oh-so-American-dream recovery that the article would have been rejected without, an article pockmarked with enough humour to keep things light, protecting reader from the boredom and reality of depression with its references to dead celebrities and hapless Tinder missives.

It was hard now to recall what I'd written, only fragments of CBT, medication, questionnaires, morsels of hope. I wrote about the domino effect of loss, its knock on, ongoing nature, and John, the losing of him, its impact, which Rebecca doubtlessly recalled from reading earlier.

I remembered it now, the time after it was published, long before I'd moved to the Lorraine Estate or Mum had returned to Ireland, how I drank in the likes and comments and messages with not a bit of catharsis, playing the role of a man who'd felt it all the same.

'It was a lovely piece,' she said, with a light smile, the bangle on her wrist jangling as she sat slightly forward.

'Thanks,' I said, awkward under praise. 'Another Aperol Spritz?'

'How about a kiss?'

'Oh my,' I said. 'I don't know if they make those here, wha–'

'Shut up, Murphy.'

Rebecca kissed me. It was just as well, as I was on the verge of saying sorry.

Conversations between soon-to-be-lovers echo elevator and pre-meeting small talk; weather and holidays, have-you-ever-been-tos and weekend plans, likes and dislikes, I've-not-been to the cinema in ages; polite interludes between the shedding of clothes and the communion of limb and skin.

Ours, however, were interspersed with the *Peep Show* episode Rebecca put on after inviting me upstairs outside her front door. Super Hans made a joke about Coldplay and the Nazis.

'Take your top off,' said Rebecca.

We kissed for some time, and then Rebecca said 'Let's put on some music' so we did, and I kissed her again, and then she took off her bra, and I kissed her there and there, and she sounded like she was having a lovely time.

She reciprocated – I was having a lovely time – and then when I thought perhaps I was going to have sex for the first time since before Donald Trump had taken office (a sadly memorable benchmark) Rebecca giggled, turned her back to me, and pulled my hand around her body.

Her skin felt good next to mine. I was unlonely. She turned to face me.

'Is this okay?' she said, the fact she'd to ask saddening to me. What if I had said no?

I nodded.

'Do I have to be big spoon though?'

She nodded.

'You do.'

'Okey dokey,' I said, at which point she turned off *Peep Show* and said 'Let's get some sleep', but had music on still, low, and a fan too for the noise, or because of the heat, I wasn't sure.

In the morning, I walked home, past carnage, an upturned bin, its innards strewn like intestines, a mix of kebab and plastic bag and banana peel suggesting a fox had gotten to it, though I doubted it'd turned the bin over in the first place. It hadn't the thumbs.

It was early, eight or so, and she had smiled at me and said she'd to get ready for work, adding 'I'll sweat the night out in the studio.'

I walked, warmed by the thought of her skin on mine, how she'd invited me home, kissed me muchly, changed her mind, or revealed the misconceptions of my own. I'd to be fine with it, and I was.

I'd a nice little giggle to myself, and warm thoughts of warm skin and held bodies, as I veered towards the Lorraine Estate.

It was 08:04.

Chapter Fifteen

- *Murphy gets political by insisting on the apolitical*
- *The media circus comes to town*
- *Murphy tells Stephen a story about Fox News, Hezbollah and more*
- *Murphy convinces himself he's on the right path*

The Purser's Retainer was thriving. They came in all shapes and sizes, some for the peace, others the novelty. A fair rake of people came via word of mouth, or after reading the in-flight magazine feature, others still the follow-ups that followed in the English media; a Guardian feature (naturally), an *Evening Standard* spread, an op-ed in *The Times* that asked if *London's First Silent Pub* had *Gone Too Far?*

The Telegraph labelled it metropolitan and socialist nonsense, the *Daily Mail* asked for an interview, *The Sun* too; both were politely refused on moral grounds, which had me a cause célèbre with the left a couple of weeks there.

Meanwhile, the men's jacks were soon plastered head to toe in stickers of various and incoherent views, loyalties, persuasions; *Free Palestine. Eat Vegan. Vote Corbyn. Level-42. Clapton Ultras. The Yeovil Seven. Gay Gooners. People's Vote. Say No to*

Murphy Who Talks

Carp. Safe Gigs for Women. St Pauli Gegen Rechts.
It wouldn't do.

The Purser's Retainer couldn't stand for politics. Stances are bad for business, unless the stance is the business itself. An *I Want to Be in EU* sticker on the cistern met my scraper, an Antifa badge and a Free the Islington One sticker too. Even the benign Lincoln FC 'Up the Imps' sticker had to go, along with all statements, gestures, points of view.

Stephen needed no convincing.

'Looks grubby. I don't want politics in here,' he said, in the belief that silence was apolitical, not politics in its most lethal form.

'Absolutely, Stephen,' I replied. 'The Purser's is a haven from the news, a bulwark against all the hate and toil of the outside world.'

'Erm, yes.'

'Like Chad Wilson from Somerville, Massachusetts.'

Stephen looked out of the window, desperate that Mr. Handley or a postman might enter and pull him away.

'Go on, Murphy.'

So I did.

'We worked together in Boston one summer. Massachusetts.'

'As opposed to?'

'Lincolnshire.'

'Of course.'

'It was the early noughties,' I said, and Stephen said 'Go on' again, used now to the fact that letting me drone on was, beyond all logic, the quickest way.

A Murphy to my Donnelly.

'His mum was a Republican,' I said. 'Dad Democrat. They'd go at each other like the clappers, not in the procreational sense, if you get me?'

'I get you.'

'Not shagging.'

'I said I got you, Murphy.'

'Brilliant stuff,' I said, with a real-life winky face too. 'So anyway, Chad worked at the same university bookstore as me, and this was around the time Israel went knocking on Lebanon's door, spraying all manner of hell around; bullets, shells and the like. Peak Bush era.'

'Uh huh.'

'So he'd all manner of trouble at home; Mum praising the Israelis, Dad saying no good came from two democracies going toe to toe, Mum calling Lebanon a terror state, that sort of carry on.'

'And?'

'Well of course it was chaos then, words like fascist and liberal and weakling and jerk-off thrown around willy-nilly, a couple married nigh on twenty years eating the faces off one another. Not in the romantic sense.'

'At least they were talking,' said Stephen, plaintively I'd say.

The coffee machine made a chugging sound, the way it did every two hours for reasons we didn't understand.

'And then what?' said Stephen.

'Good question, sir. Chad was a smart lad, with no idea if Israel was wrong, Lebanon wrong, or the pair of them right and wrong altogether. But he knew a thing that was right without doubt.'

'Which was?'

'That everyone in the Wilson household needed to drink a nice, big cup of shut the fuck up.'

'I see,' said Stephen, adding 'So...?'

I went on.

'So he banned all conversation from the dinner table. No words, nothing. No shooting the shit over baseball, no work talk, war talk, politics talk; no Bush, Hezbollah, Fox, NBC, CBN or CBS. They couldn't even discuss the weather.'

'Sounds a bit severe,' said Stephen. 'What was the result?'

'Harmony,' I said. 'Well, that was the case in 2006. I've not heard from him since then. They might be dead, divorced or both for all I know.'

Stephen nodded.

'Go refill the ice, Murphy.'

'Capital idea, sir,' I said, and did, though before I went I looked around the quiet of our pub, saw the contented faces of the people with their silently ordered pints and wines, teas and coffees and, though I had enjoyed myself the evening before, still believed I had created a sort of heaven on the ground, with decent crisps to boot.

Chapter Sixteen

- *The 2018 FIFA World Cup in Russia begins in earnest*
- *Murphy (sort of) talks back to Donnelly**
- *The Purser's Retainer gets a noise complaint of all things*
- *Love*

* very sort of

There was a carnivalistic atmosphere in the air, London buoyant, stuffy, hopeful and expectant. The summer had arrived. There was a football thing on too.

Russia had won, as had Uruguay.

I've the telly on and the Kindle on the go, my mother wrote of reading and football, leading me to believe retirement was grand.

Since that night at Rebecca's, I had begun to see her often. She told me she'd no interest in a relationship, but asked me around most nights, one in every two, all the same. If I wasn't at work in the day, and she wasn't, she'd ask me if I wanted to come over. So I'd go, purely for the betterment of yoga, as she'd said 'There is a need for drastic improvement', and I would stretch. Then sometimes *we*.

Murphy Who Talks

This is a novel.

Shy, retiring, sexually repressed men with waists migrating west and east can get it on with their yoga teachers. Yoga teachers can shit themselves for caffeine and smoke cigarettes and do whatever and be with whoever the hell they like without the judgement that comes from it. It's a novel.

But the stuff with Russia and Uruguay did happen.

Iran beat the Moroccans. That happened. Spain and Portugal played out a three all draw, that happened too, I remember it well, because I watched it with Con Connelly and Donnelly, the events of which I will soon recount.

For the first time in a long time I'd a routine; yoga by day, work by night, or the other way around. I would work my hours, go to class and then see Rebecca, waltzing down the litter-strewn streets of Holloway Road, past the Emirates Stadium, towards the small flat where she lived with two others near Arsenal station.

The noise was the same as ever but it wasn't.

The cars beeped but didn't bother me the same. People shouted but it was more music than noise. I wanted peace and quiet still but, during those fifteen-minute walks, with the football thing on, the heat in the air, it was like I was on the inside of what it meant to be living.

I was in Erin's Rejoinder with Donnelly and Con Connelly. Con had been working on a site in King's Cross, Don at his office nearby, me at The Purser's Retainer. After my evening out with Rebecca, I had told Don that I'd *just wanted an early night*, to which he'd replied *what's his name?* and when I said it would have been John Senior's birthday that day he replied to say *ah, fair enough.*

It was not. John's birthday was later in the month. Lying felt good.

During my shift, a neighbour oblivious to the nature of our pub had come in to complain about noise.

'An absolute racket,' he said, to which I said, 'Positively absolutely completely utterly sorry kindly, sir,' and promised that we would try to keep it down.

'See that you do,' said the man, mid-sixties, haughty as fuck you might say.

He left. Stephen returned from a meeting; bank, Tinder, gym, I never knew what it was he was up to outside of the pub.

'Stephen, we had a noise complaint.'

'How is that possible?' he said, looking around the busy-ish pub, quiet as a mouse, quieter even than Mickey, who now that I thought about it was still likely trapped in his final resting place downstairs. I certainly hadn't emptied the traps of late.

'It isn't,' I said. 'It was the Eritrean café up the road. Peace deal with Ethiopia. Fireworks into the night. Hugs and kisses. Shisha and smiles. They were at it all hours. Beautiful sight.'

'But why did he think it was us?'

'We're a pub.'

'But we're a silent pub.'

'I don't think he's on the Snap That, Stephen,' I said, and he asked if I explained, and I said 'No, I just told him what he wanted to hear.'

'Fair enough, would you ever pass me a pack of Taytos?'

'Cheese & Onion?

'Naturally.

The world was shaping up just as I wanted it. It was scorching hot out, the sweet scent of tarmac filling the London air with every intake of breath. The World Cup filtered out thoughts the way radiators, kettles, radios and conversations did silence for Rebecca.

Murphy Who Talks

Sitting in the pub now, I showed Donnelly the dating profiles he'd helped curate; my active picture, my arm around one friend picture, my smiling without looking like a serial killer picture.

I'd even matched with and spoken to a couple of girls only to show Don I was doing what he wanted. If I'm being honest, I'd no intention to meet them, so you might say I led them on, even if couching it under terms like innocent chatter and lighthearted conversation.

They'd no idea.

'Any kindling? Murphy,' he said, after we sat down in Erin's Rejoinder to watch Portugal thump Spain or Spain thump Portugal, drawn to the same pub as always through familiarity, Donnelly's contempt for crowds, Con's desire to sit down after a long, hard day on his knees.

'No kindling,' I said, sipping my pint.

'What about the Rachel girl you showed me?' said Donnelly. 'She was fit.'

'She was,' I said. 'But she gave me the unmatch. Didn't like the one I told about the short-sighted longshoreman with the shallow breaths.'

Donnelly exhaled, held up two pinched fingers.

'Remember what I said, Murphy.'

'Don't be yourself?'

'Exactly. Don't be yourself, Murphy.'

'Brilliant stuff,' I said, sipping again on my pint.

Donnelly never spoke of his own life, pushing conversations away from himself and onto others (me for the most part), even though there were evenings when he was absent without explanation, when he didn't respond on the same WhatsApp thread he was militantly glued to most of the time.

It was fun to lie, easy too. To sip my pint, tell 'em what they wanted to hear when, in my mind, I knew, were I to switch on the data, I might find company there.

Goldie fell over again today she might write, or *Irene put crystals out in her class again. They're from the Congo ffs.*

The man with the boobs is at my half twelve class, was there during one furtive glance, along with *Pray for me*, to which I wrote a quick *cop a look for me*, and she *that's gross*, and me *absofupping-lutely. Now stop perving on your students.*

'kay.

The boys were used to my being alone. It'd been the status quo since my return to London, induced by 'a difficult episode', a return that yielded calls from *here* to *there* as the pair of us tried to 'make it work', in denial as I was to the reality that you've to live *there* if the pair of you are to call home *here*, to be together in so many words.

An episode through which Donnelly and Connelly had been present in my life at times, and absent also, when they'd their own to live though, to Donnelly's unfortunate credit, as I said, he'd a habit of putting his to one side at the most inconveniently important of times.

During our childhood I'd never had a girlfriend, and not at university either, so my being single was nothing new to Donnelly or Con. When I was introverted and mullsome neither man thought a thing of it, just as they thought nothing when I'd try and ward off Donnelly with the one about the eejit Marcus who'd all the sense of a solar panel farm in West Cork.

'Shut up, Murphy,' said Donnelly, after I had said just that.

Order was restored.

They saw nothing unusual in the conversation drifting towards someone else either, namely Con, who had himself been on a Tinder date the previous week, telling us he'd had a nice time.

Murphy Who Talks

'How nice a time?' said Donnelly.

Con answered honestly.

Said too that he was unsure if it was a goer, unsure if he wanted to date her again, date her a while, or not date her at all. Naturally, Don had a simpler take on the matter.

'She has tits,' he said, a grin on him, needling one at that. 'She has a fanny. What more do you want?'

I looked at Donnelly, his grin a curious mix of aggression and facetious innocence; the contours erected to kid the likes of us that it was just craic, a little fun. A nothing.

'*Honest* to God, Don' I said. He looked surprised. Con too. 'Cop on, will you,' I said.

I regretted my phrasing immediately. For if women had no counties, what Donnelly was guilty of had no borders, and I wished to focus on that, only I'd given him reason to mock and dismiss, thereby distracting us from the issue.

Initially shocked, he soon smiled, finding opportunity in my choice of words.

'Alright,' he said. 'Calm down Paddy O'Plastic.'

Order, hierarchy and the damned status quo were restored.

Resigned, I turned to Con.

'Will you see her again?' I asked, and imagined he would have given an honest answer, but he was let off by a football man named Nacho, who did a goal, such that the pub went mad, and we clapped, and we cheered, and we watched the replay the three times that it was played and forgot about honest answers altogether.

I sipped my pint. If I'd had a pair of stones, I'd have called Don out more often, but I didn't. I was a coward, see; a pity that, because while I was wrong often and to some minds most of the time, on this topic I was *right*.

Donnelly did not talk nicely about girls.

Or boys. But if he was snaky with how he talked about

lads, it was girls who got the venom; cold-hearted, thoughtless man that he was, or could be.

I looked at the table, where Donnelly had ripped open a pack of (Catholic) Taytos, making a mess on the floor, the oak, the stools. I told him as much. He laughed, so did I, a triviality. But to chastise the way he talked about women was different. It went to the core of us both, such that we'd get defensive, me saying something weak along the lines of 'Come on, Donnelly', him replying with 'You're just jealous, Murphy', which, though beside the point, had often been so unfortunately true.

Tits and fanny was far from the worst of it. There were times when tits were breasts, jubblies or melons. Those were the days when his day had gone well.

'I don't want to get caught up in that MeToo business,' he'd say on those days, talking of women, hushed tones feigned, intentionally audible.

'It was a fairly big business, Don,' I would try, getting rolled eyes for my efforts, caustic laughter, claims that I was a Johnny Right-On, a Group Think Do-Gooder, Donnelly speaking loud enough and often enough and dismissively enough that on occasion, after enough browbeating, you'd the feeling that maybe he was right.

But those were the good days, when he was immature, dismissive and unthinking.

On other days, tits were tits as we'd somehow not a word for them hateful.

But fanny was cunt on those days, a harsh word at the end of hard-nosed harsh days at the office, when to say 'Come off it, Donnelly' would be met only with 'Not now, Murphy,' or 'Give it a rest, Murphy' or worst of all 'Here he goes…'

I looked at the Taytos, the pack finished, morsels everywhere, aluminium packet ripped wide open but still clear as

Murphy Who Talks

to what it was, a pack of Cheese & Onion (naturally) Taytos eaten, enjoyed, empty of content but Taytos all the same.

When Donnelly was Donnelly at the end of long, hard-nosed days, women weren't women weren't girls weren't much more than things; less than a pack of Taytos, which could still say it was a pack of Taytos, albeit empty.

I hated the way he was but hated the way I was more still; silent, passive and tacitly yielding.

There were days when *she* had *only* tits and a fanny, more days still when she'd *only* a cunt and tits, such that in its harshness she became not a thing with a cunt but just a *pair* of tits and a cunt itself, less than a bag of crisps which, when stripped, still had a semblance of itself. I had tried with Donnelly, ever since school, since the trinity of us had sat together in form, Year 9, I had tried. But never quite enough. I preferred my friendship with its flaws.

On the occasions when I did, Donnelly used the one weapon he had against me, the thing I loved; words, his harsh and caustic, buzzwordy and topical, ones he'd appropriated so as not to face up the realities of himself.

'Have I triggered you, Murphy?' he'd say, or 'Shall I check my privilege, Murphy?' or, when all else had failed, he would use privilege against me. 'The last time I checked, Murphy, you were a privileged white man too'.

There was no denying that.

Most of all though, I avoided conflict with him, and he did with me. But if all else failed, he'd another line to keep me in my place.

'Shut up, Murphy.'

It worked every time.

You might say he was no friend, but he was only playing with the tools he had to hand; to bark when kettled, to use my flaws against me in order to avoid mining his own, to shine a light on me if it meant he didn't have to take a closer look at himself; I was lonely so I was jealous, I was conflict-averse so I was weak; I never got laid, rarely dated, kissed or flirted with women.

I was hung up over Karolina in a way that made Romeo seem non-committal.

I was incapable, and it went unaddressed, Don needling me to *try harder*, even though we both knew I hadn't it in me to be anything other than what I was; Murphy O'Meekly.

'Thing is, Murphy,' he had once said. 'Women want vulnerable and sensitive men. Just not *their* men.'

I nodded, unsure, and thought he was trying to help, only for him to grin, look me in the eye and say, 'So stop being a fanny.'

The game ended in a draw, suppressed male thought erupting via a late equaliser, men who knew each other too well to hug hugging, men who didn't know each other well enough to hug hugging also.

I asked the boys if they wanted a final pint and they said yes and I walked up and ordered three Amstels at the bar.

I envied Donnelly. Words were nothing to him.

The barmaid was a barmaid, Donnelly Donnelly, Taytos Taytos, the pub the pub. The three pints of Amstel were three pints of Amstel, which I had in my hand, just as the matted chewing gum on the patterned carpet was what it was. Karolina was Karolina, but not mine, anymore, which hurt, 'til I remembered words didn't mean a thing no more.

As such, hurt no longer hurt.

All the same, I knew I didn't want to be like Donnelly.

It seemed so much simpler to him, the past a word, cunt, tits, just words, fanny, breasts just words too, women people he could love, 'til he'd to convince himself and the world he didn't, so as to make them only words. Mary, Christina, O'Leary, Maddox. Words now, nothing more.

I was oft mullsome and over-thinking about it all. That much was true. Don was a dick. So was that. And I needed him, and that was a trinity of truths, so to make a square of the matter I buried my head in the sand; a needy coward.

I looked up at my phone. Rebecca was teaching her evening class now. I looked at Twitter, then up at Con and Don. Later that evening, in Rebecca's room, I would try to do as she instructed, after having said I'd a needling pain in my back.

'You will snap,' she said, from the other side of the room.

'Not at all,' I said. 'I'm getting better with every class. I'm as supple as water.'

I lowered 'til it was almost on the floor, a slight bridge in my lumbar leaving a gap between my tramp-stamp region and the parquet.

'You have a spider web on the cornice of your ceiling,' I said.

'I don't like spiders,' said Rebecca. 'Do you want to get rid of it?'

'Oh, I can't do that,' I said. 'He's as much right to live there as you do here.'

'He doesn't pay rent.'

'But he hasn't invested himself in the wage-labour system the way you *have*, Rebecca,' I said. 'So you can't be saying Mr. Spider you've no right to be here, because you're not the landlord any more than he is. You'd best learn to live with Mr. Spider. I'll not be removing spiders because you're afraid of them.'

Slow, sticky footsteps told me Rebecca was approaching before I saw her looking down at me.

'That's very sexist, Murphy. I never said I was afraid of

spiders. I said I didn't like them.'

'Sorry,' I said.

A pause.

'You're damn right sorry,' she said, by way of confirmation.

'You've got the run of me there,' I said. 'I'm a throw-back, a tiresome old–'

'Fool.' She stepped a little closer. 'Now if you won't help me remove the twat spider, I'll do it myself.'

'You're worse than Rachman.'

'Who?'

'Never mind. Help me up and I'll get rid of the arachnid squatter.'

She smiled.

'What's wrong, Murphy?'

'Nothing,' I said. 'I just pine for those supple fingers around my tender, fixed-firm form.'

'You can't get up, can you?'

'I can.'

'Go on then.'

I couldn't get up.

'Belligerence doesn't suit you, Murphy,' said Rebecca.

Kneeling on the floor, she held me in her arms, supple maybe, dead weight perhaps.

I've to admit it was good so, to be held there, but with perverse inversion I felt the need to cut through the danger of intimacy, so I said 'Kiss me, Hardy', and she laughed a little, then did.

That was all later though, but right now I'd lofty thoughts of how I was perfect and Donnelly was not, how he was wrong to my right, in totality, without the nuances between us.

At the same time, I did want to get the rise off him for the ways that he often, and oftener more these days, was. So I did.

Murphy Who Talks

'Did I ever tell you lads about Benny Wrench from Colchester, who lost his job at Twitter?'

'Shut up, Murphy.'

'He was mad upset, said he'd miss the office, full of characters.'

'Shut up, Murphy.'

'All one hundred and twenty of them.'

'Murphy,' he said, and, in fairness, had some laugh in him. 'Do. Shut. Up.'

I winked at Con. It was easier this way. I turned to Donnelly. 'What about you Don boy, any scandal in your life?'

It was just after nine.

Chapter Seventeen

- *Murphy and his mother discuss the literature of Olivia Sudjic*
- *Murphy gets colonial*
- *Murphy reflects on a stolen youth*

The French edged the Aussies and the Danes Peru, and Iceland were delighted with a goal against Argentina but Argentina horrified with only one against them, such is the nature of culture and historic expectation. Croatia beat Nigeria, the Serbs Costa Rica and the Mexicans Germany, the only surprise there that I was no longer surprised by surprises.

You'd need to be blind.

Brazil played the Swiss and scored the one goal, but the Swiss scored one too, and what with expectancy and history, you could say it was like the Swiss had beaten Brazil.

Are you out and about? Mum's message read, as I sat in the heat of my room, windows open, the noise of angry traffic on the street.

I am meeting a friend, was my reply, met itself with *What's her name?*

Eh?

You've not said Declan (Donnelly) *or Connor, and you don't have any other friends.*

She was, as always, to the point. In this instance, she had one too.

Indeed, I wrote.

Are you going to tell me then?

I'm not, no. How's Cashel?

Fine, she wrote, maybe answering maybe not. *Your father kept me hidden from your grandmother eight months. But he was at sea.*

The conversation moved on. I asked my mother if she'd enjoyed the book I'd posted.

Sympathy?

That's the one. Did you like it?

Yes, but I couldn't make head nor tail of the Instagram stuff.

I laughed, walking along the Holloway Road, wrote *That's the plot*, and almost tripped over a man sat crossed leg on the floor, with a cardboard CV and a Costa cup bank account.

Well, I guess the plot passed me by then, Mum wrote, adding that she had *enjoyed it all the same.*

Good, that's the main thing. I'd best be going

Go go. Have a lovely evening.

And yourself, I wrote, with an *x* for love and another *x* for good measure.

There was a large group of students sitting at a long table in The Regional Pickpocket, where I was watching the England Tunisia match with Con and Donnelly, the three of us venturing out from our usual haunt, sucked in, you might say, by the enthusiasm and euphoria that sat uneasily in me, the festooned flags inside and outside the bar, the people with their faces painted white and red, the songs sang so mindlessly as to be almost innocent.

Some of the students had drinks, others not. Had they been in The Purser's Retainer, I'd have had Stephen write them a note informing them to buy drinks or get the hell out.

It was a business, not a sixth form common room.

I had grasped after Ireland, and pushed England away, yet here I was, drawn by a lifelong love of football, the magnetic appeal of the FIFA World Cup in Russia, and the fact the country was still very much unsure if it was coming or going, if it was itself here or there.

That was how I reasoned it anyway, me, not English, a bit English, full English English, my pink and pale arse sat on a wooden stool in a pub devoid of Celtic cross, county scarf or Tricolour, or those strange, metal Proclamation of Independence etchings you tended to see in our pubs, alongside epithets like Home is Where the Heart is or I Drink Therefore I Am.

Instead, here I was, the red and the white on bunting and flags and women and men.

It was almost like I wanted it to be home.

Only I couldn't accept that, so I'd to push it away.

'Heineken?' I asked the boys, upon finding them sat at a small table at the back of the bar. They both nodded. I went up to the bar and got the drinks.

It was 18:45.

The Regional Pickpocket was large, with a high ceiling and parquet floors, the kind of pub that asked itself if it wanted to display the flag of St. George in April, during World Cups, or not at all.

It had festooned itself with blue and red and white for the

Murphy Who Talks

Royal Wedding, but while the innocent white and blood red of St. George had connotations, the red, white and blue of the Union Jack did not, unless you were from the Aden Protectorate, Anglo-Egyptian Sudan, Malta or the Bahamas, Bahrain, Sri Lanka nee Ceylon, Balleland or Bangladesh or Barbados, Basutoland, Bechuanaland–

'Murphy.'

'*Or* Bermuda or British Borneo. East Africa, Egypt, Guiana, Honduras, Malaya, the Solomon Islands, Somaliland–'

'Murphy.'

'Burma, Colonial Fiji, *Ireland*, Nauru, Togola–'

'Murphy!'

I turned to my right. It was Con of all people.

'What?'

'Will you shut up? The teams are in.'

'The Seychelles is another one,' I said and 'Let's not forget Australia as a whole' and was about to add 'There's the Sultanate of Zanzibar,' but he glared at me, said 'Coming here was your idea' and I'd no choice but to admit this was true, and settle into an uncomfortable, homely comfort to watch the game.

It was 18:51.

After all was said and done, I wanted to be out and about, amongst the people, the crisp-ignorant, flag-waving British, with their misread history and their complicated pride; to dip my toe into their pool, see what it was like to be inside of it all.

I could have worked that night. Stephen had given me the option. But I chose to watch the game under the guise of friendship and football when, in truth, it was England, and England above all, I wanted to watch, if only to see how they got on, picking a pub with craft beer and parquet flooring, with customers that had straight backs and genuine smiles, a pub where the pub quiz was a night out rather than a refuge from life.

Maybe I could support England after all, and Ireland too. Maybe it didn't mean I'd to eat Victoria Sponge or sing that anthem or believe the myths of Arthur and Churchill or eat curry or claim the Falklands as my or our own. Maybe I could just be English, a bit English, or not English at all and still support that team without being needled by its bloodred and purist white flag.

That, or The Olive Branch had made me want to spend my life in nicer pubs and bars. Under the heat of June's unforgiving sun, London's roads shimmered 'neath refracted light, the line between distraction and truth blurred in pubs with projectors and parks giant tellies that made people ants.

In an age when you'd to be *something*, I'd convinced myself I was outside of it all.

But as we sat there, three mongrels, blending in or out as we saw fit, I knew we'd had a place at the table for many years.

England beat Tunisia two to one, a half-English or full-English but certainly not no English Irishman scoring one of the goals. Con was pleased. Donnelly less so. He felt England should have won by more.

Students sang 'Three Lions' and pronounced *Jules Rimet still gleaming* as *Jewells Remain*.

Donnelly shook his head, saying 'Idiots,' to which I said 'Ah Don, they're kids' adding 'leave them be, they're only young.'

He snorted derisively.

'So are we.'

I wasn't so sure. To my mind, others had put paid to that. I pointed to our near-empty glasses. 'Same again?'

They nodded, and I went to the bar.

It was 21:09.

Murphy Who Talks

Chapter Eighteen

- *Pets for the homeless!*
- *Silence for the pub*
- *The hamster wheel of life*

Colombia had lost to Japan and Poland Senegal.

Uruguay beat the Saudis while the Danes and Australians drew.

Anyone who cared had wrapped themselves in the World Cup's nostalgic warm glow, its twists and turns, like spindling oak-tree roots, a respite from day-to-day life, the chaos of radio, telly, screens and feeds.

The pub was doing well, silence going swimmingly, hashtags about us floating around here, there and everywhere, punters floating in, playing by the rules, a delight to see.

Only we'd a problem.

While I had succeeded in creating a quiet refuge where I could watch the games, I had no control over the outside world, namely, the homeless.

It would set us back about two hundred quid.

I suppose you might say the issue had begun with kindness, though I'd argue it began with the giving of a cigarette and nothing more.

One sunny morning a few months earlier, whilst doing my usual round of the pub's exterior, I looked up from my brush and broom to find a woman looking at me. It was Welsh Jess, who had come from Swansea years earlier, squatted and screwed and been screwed over, and was now living on hard times.

'Got a quid, Murphy?' she asked. 'I'm trying to get into a hostel tonight.'

In my defence, I had no cash on me, but for the reasons of insecurity and poor character, hadn't it in me to just say no.

'I don't,' I said. 'By which I mean I can't. If I give you the pound, I've to give Donald here the pound, and it wouldn't be fair on Jack (an ex-seaman from Wrexham) and I'd feel inclined to help out Curtis (from Dalston, via Kingston, in Jamaica, not upon-Thames). And given I'm only on £7.38 an hour, before you know it, I'd be out of pocket.'

I looked at her looking at me, confusion in her eyes, and felt a pang of pained pity.

'Will you take a snout?' I asked.

'Yeah, okay,' she said.

Her friends, nearby, looked on, such that I'd an inclination to offer the cigarettes around. They took them gratefully. And so this went on for four days, such that I doled out sixteen cigarettes from a pack that cost thirteen pounds, spending more on generosity borne of guilt than if I'd just gone to a cash machine in the first place.

It became a mainstay of my working week, and I had made my peace with that, only we had an issue now that needed to be resolved.

Neither me nor Stephen (we'll not talk of Mr. Handley) had minded the homeless people hanging around when the pub was a relic dying a slow death, Stephen too craven or decent to say anything, me enjoying a chat as I did my rounds or had my cigarette, which is not to romanticise the matter. They hadn't freight-train tales nor pap poetry as gentlemen (and gentlewoman) of the road. They'd shitty lives, but were friendly skins, and whilst I tried to avoid people for the most part, I felt disinclined to avoid those avoided by everyone else. But it wasn't about me anymore. We'd a business to run.

The USP of the Purser's was running up against our neighbours' uncouth but inalienable rights to free speech and association, and we'd to do something about it. If the pub became a Pret, there was no way the homeless people could hang around outside. They were sure to be moved along. So I'd to find a way to help them as much as to help us. If I said that to myself enough, I could almost believe my own bullshit reasoning. But still, something had to be done.

We couldn't just round them up and cart them off. Sure, we were turkeys voting for Christmas, watching a football tournament playing out in a gangster's paradise, but back then we'd the sheen at least of a country with sanity and norms.

I had allowed sentiment to get the better of me, and now it was affecting business, and I'd to find a way that would both help the homeless people as well as see them move along.

I needed to find a way to make them human.

Cuddly animals would be my answer.

'What are we going to do?' Stephen said, a few days after the England Tunisia game. The homeless people were making a hell of a noise.

'About what?'

'About the homeless.'

'People,' I said.

'What?'

'Homeless people, Stephen.'

'That's what I said.'

'No, you said homeless.'

'Enough, Murphy, what are we going to do about the homeless people?'

I looked out of the window. The usual crowd of young, old, dirty, clean, on crutches, in good physical shape, scowling, smiling, drunk, sober, high, low and somewhere in between were hanging around in front of The Purser's Retainer as they had been for the weeks, the reality of them shone upon us now that we'd done away with the Spotify playlists and as much noise as was possible within the confines of our pub, my decision to converse whilst sweeping or watering the plants coming back to haunt me.

They did no harm, of course, though the noise was discordant, Donald the retired lorry driver the worst, with his habit of laughing loudly and jackal like as he worked through a can of K and, if he'd baccy on him, a weak drum-lite roll-up cigarette.

Sure, there was the constant drone of cars, the hammer of hammers, and the drill of drills at the Grayling Estate. But that was progress, building work, houses gleaming towards a brighter future. The homeless (people) were a stasis, and though I pitied them, I couldn't pity them to the extent that it damaged our business. Punters were happy to sit in silence in The Purser's Retainer, enjoying the sound of passing Honda Garibaldis and drilling drills.

But Donald's shrill, hyena-like laugh, or an argument between Curtis and Jack over who'd left washing on the tent they shared beside the Sobell Leisure Centre wasn't good for peace, business either.

So I'd to come up with a plan.

'Can we not just call the police?' Stephen said.

Murphy Who Talks

'Not possible,' I said. 'They're stretched enough as it is.'

'But they're loitering. Isn't that against the law?'

'Maybe yes, maybe no, maybe not maybe so,' I said, and before Stephen could say more I reminded him that, given the CPO we still had hanging over us, it was in the interests of the police to have one less anti-social pub in the area, more facilities that might serve the Grayling estate with no social aspect at all, such that we were best off not having the police snooping around if at all possible.

'I take your point,' said Stephen. 'What are we going to do? Maybe offer to buy them food and politely ask them to *loiter* down the road?'

'Stephen if we give them food, they'll only spend it on drugs.'

'That doesn't make any sense.'

'What does these days?'

A Nissan Chimera with a spoiler 'neath its body roared by on the Seven Sisters Road.

'Stephen, if we want to unburden ourselves of the homeless [people], the only sensible, logical thing we can do is to give them pets.'

'Pets!?'

'Yes,' I said. 'Homeless people like pets, just as normal people like pets. And pets elicit empathy, pity, and cold, hard cash.'

'Sounds unethical.'

'Now you're catching on,' I said.

And so we became the first pub to *obtain* pets for the homeless, such that Donald had a kitten called Craig, Welsh Jess a puppy she named Spot, Jack a guinea pig called Clyde and Curtis, because it was the only animal my supplier had left, a ferret he named Watson, for reasons I never did discover.

And they loved us for it.

But in spite of their ears, noses, hearts, feet, hands, faces, hopes, dreams, hurts and disappointments, the homeless were not people, so they were not the public, so the public had a different view about it, which was that the public were aghast.

Including Rebecca.

I was a human surfboard.

As per usual, I was meant to be practising my poses, gaming the system a little, extra-curricular tutoring to unpick the innate disadvantages I had by dint of bad genes and a lifestyle yet worse.

But in all its rigidity, my back was nothing compared to the intractability of Rebecca's views on the matter.

I'd told her about the pets, the homeless, how in giving them sentient charity boxes we'd tapped into the oft-dormant nature of human pity. But Rebecca was a member of the public, and like the average member of the public, she was not happy.

Literally and figuratively, she was on my back about what we'd done up at The Purser's Retainer, curling her toes with malicious intent.

'Murphy! Promise me you'll take those poor creatures away and put them somewhere safe.'

'A shelter?'

'Yes.'

'Crisis? St. Mungo's?' I squeezed out, between struggled breaths. She curled her toes, full locust much harder with a 5'6" blonde woman on the small of your back, her feet pressing into what seemed less lumbar, more the depths of my soul.

'The animals, Murphy! Those poor creatures!'

'You sound like my gran,' I said, struggling through the pain – and pleasure – of her toes, knots unfurling with each movement, the net benefit of her torture evident later that day

Murphy Who Talks

but, at the time, second to the physical pain, and our diverging points of view.

'Murphy, I am not joking,' said Rebecca. 'It's cruel to give homeless people pets.'

I flailed, like a beached whale.

'*Vraiment!*'

'You don't speak French, Murphy.'

'*Fakt?*'

She stood on the end of her toes (awkward pose), her balance impressive given my general pudge. The pain was intense, electrifying, agonising also, and I yelped, much like Spot the Dog.

'Murphy, it's not responsible to give homeless people animals to look after. They find it hard enough to look after themselves.'

'It's company.'

'It's responsibility.'

'It's companionship.'

'It's dangerous.'

'It's visible.'

She lowered her toes, so she was now just standing on the small of my back, an improvement in relative terms. I stopped flailing.

'Murphy, I understand you are trying to help,' she said, sitting down on my back.

'Aarf aarf,' I said, unsure what sound a beached whale made.

'I *understand* you are trying to help. Or at least I think that's what you're trying to do. It's never fully clear. But this is not the way.' She hadn't, I noted, denied that pets made homeless people visible, nor that without them they were not.

'It's working,' I said.

This much was true. Since obtaining animal companions

for our homeless friends, the public had responded in kind.

They had judged.

They had complained.

Like Rebecca, they'd said it was wrong for a ferret named Watson to live under the charge of a homeless man named Curtis, because he was a ferret, rather than because he'd been named Watson, I believe. They said it was *cruel, wrong, careless* and best of all *inhumane* and yet, in doing so, they took out their wallets and gave the homeless great wads of cash, enough to make Croesus blush. They'd no idea it was me who'd gotten the animals. I told the homeless lads I'd done so illegally, made them promise not to say a word, and we'd gotten off scot-free. The homeless now had money, but wherever they spent the money, it wasn't in The Purser's Retainer. More than welcome as they were (they could be punters now, after all), they likely assumed that they were not, or were unwilling to pay our grossly inflated (Because London) prices.

Whatever they spent their money on, I've no idea, though when I did see the animals they were all in rude health, so it appeared money had solved the problem, that the homeless people had acted as human people too, given the tools which, in many – though not all – cases was simply a case of money; nothing else.

It was that simple.

'Okay,' I told Rebecca. 'I'll see if I can't get them to give their pets to the RSPCA or something.'

Her parquet floor was cold to the touch, a relief on such a hot day.

'Good,' she said, and that was all.

Though I didn't ultimately do as she asked, soon enough the pets were taken all the same, an unfounded rumour spreading that Lucy had got Spot drunk, that Clyde had pinkeye and that the ferret had been introduced into the cruel but – trust me

Murphy Who Talks

– lucrative world of ferret fighting.

These things were not true, but they'd the ring of plausibility to those who needed it, which was not that they were homeless people with, by proxy, homeless pets, but that there were homeless people with pets at all, such that the pets were confiscated and put into shelters; homes.

They did not love us for it.

The homeless (people) figured us the culprits, as we'd a roof over our heads, a business to run and a reason to clear them from the streets. They thought it us that'd shopped them hanging around out front; drinking White Lightning, passing the time, scouting the pavements for fag ends with bits of tobacco, swearing at each other, saying kindnesses also.

They blamed us and they disappeared. We had, to their minds, evoked a thing in them that, finally, if the public that pushed them away had been able to see it, proved they were human after all.

Hurt.

It was then that I realised that my cause had been of ulterior motive wrapped up in the lofty. Yes, I wanted to help them, but if I'd only wanted to help I could have done so well before the Purser's became a profitable concern.

At heart, if I'm honest, I had finally a thing to believe in; purpose, a passion, a thing that meant the homeless people's presence was simply getting in the way. A colder man would have simply moved them on, a less needy one also. It's not like they weren't used to being moved on and, often enough, away.

But I needed to be loved, and I was guilty not for what I did with the pets (if the homeless were paupers, our four-legged friends were being treated like royalty) but the fact I did it to *deal* with what'd come to be not so much problematic people as much as solely a problem.

So, when I discovered they were clustering outside *The*

Jademaster's Annex at the Finsbury Park end of the Seven Sisters Road, I decided to help, genuinely and proper. Only it turns out you've to have a license to do busking in this country, such that I spent a night thereafter in the Kentish Town cells.

'Law aside, Murphy, no one wants to hear an acoustic rendition of 'Smack my Bitch Up.'

I respectfully disagreed, went on my way, and handed the fifty-seven pence earned in my set to Donald the retired lorry driver.

'Thanks Murphy,' he said. 'You're an awful singer.'

'Aye, I am. Still, at least it wasn't Bono.'

We drank to that, he a little K, me my bougie Heineken (the World Cup advertising had worked on me) by the streetside, chatting on a little while.

Murphy Who Talks

Chapter Nineteen

- *Stephen develops an entrepreneurial streak of his own, leading to utter disaster*
- *Change happens, whether Murphy likes it or not*
- *Rebecca and Murphy discuss the double standards of scatological humour*

I was in The Purser's Retainer, pub quiet, BBC on, Gary Lineker and friends analysing Croatia's drubbing of Argentina, which I had watched in blessed silence, distracted every now and then only by a customer politely writing a number on a piece of paper to tell me which tap to tap or drink to pour.

It was 21:32. Mr. Handley passed me a written note.

Blonde. Far corner. 9/10

In lieu of conversation, he'd taken to this, but as most of the punters in *London's First Silent Pub* were men, it was thankfully rare.

I looked up, peered over, and scribbled down a number, to which Mr. Handley gave me a look, as if to say 'Honestly?'

I turned the number around.

∞

I added two dots for eyes, a cartoonish nose, a smiley face, stuck out my tongue, and went to the washroom.

I checked my phone, read two texts, one from my mother, saying the *poor creatures*, the homeless, rather than the animals, the subject. My eyes rested on the words a minute, as I assessed, tried to let them sink in.

I thought, a-bit thought, then didn't think at all, distracted as I was by Rebecca's message, about the inflexible Maisie Cox, who came to her late-afternoon class, and another message that read *how's the deathly silence of the pub?*

I was about to answer when I noticed Stephen walking into the back room.

'Murphy.'

'Stephen.'

'I've had an idea.'

This was new.

'I like ideas, Stephen,' I said. 'What is it? Jerk venison, tri-fried chicory, Chinese whispers?'

'I don't think you're allowed to say that anymore,' he said.

'I was just testing you.'

'And anyway, it wouldn't be allowed in here.'

'Good man.'

Mr. Handley's laugh drifted in through the back-bar door. We allowed him three daily, after which his loyalty card was null and void, 'til six p.m.

'No,' said Stephen. 'I've realised that we don't need to show the football.'

'What?'

'People are coming in waves, which is great. But they're here for the quiet, not football.'

'What?'

'Your plan, Murphy, it really worked.'

A pause elicited the strength of my work.

'Stephen, once more now with the thing about switching off the football. Run that by me again?'

Murphy Who Talks

'It's only getting in the way,' he said, as echoes passed through the door, a Rover Explicit rumbling on the Seven Sisters Road and lifelong tinnitus the only things between me and the sound of total silence.

'But Stephen, we have the volume off on the football, and no one's cheering or shouting or raging or roaring. It's just background music, without the sound. They're coming in to see the games without all the clamour that goes with the competition.'

Stephen opened the washroom door, willing me to lead the way.

'Take a look,' was all he said.

We walked out. I was met with three cold, hard truths. It wasn't that they were all white, though they mostly were, or that they were all men, though they mostly were. There were women and there were young ones, man and woman, and there were old ones and cool ones and drab-dressed plain looking ones and happy looking ones enjoying a half pint or a no pint soft drink and sad doeeyed looking fellas hunched over and guys drawing and women reading and everything in between. And the truths?

There was not an empty seat in the house.

There was not a sound.

And there was not a soul watching the football and, much as I might say to Stephen that was because we'd the highlights on now, it had been like this for days. We returned to the washroom.

'Murphy, you've achieved something brilliant,' he said. 'The rest of the world's watching the football, everyone desperate to avoid it is here, and they're part of the world. You've given a voice to the voiceless, hope to the hopeless, seats to the formerly seatless, placeless and publess.'

He was making up words now. What in God's name had I

done?

'People want to be in on something,' he said. 'And if they're not *in* on the football watching, they want to be *in* on being *outside* of it.'

I stood still, my studiedly vacant expression now simply vacant, my affable disposition failing me. I'd created a monster, of words and italics.

'But wh–'

'They're playing board games quietly,' said Stephen. 'They're reading books. They're meditating for goodness' sake. They're *happy*.' I took another look. They were as well. 'They're here because of *you*, Murphy. Because of what you've created. However, I asked a few of them–'

I made to interject but he said, 'In writing' and I'd to nod and whisper 'Good man' to keep up appearances, all the while dying inside.

'They're all saying the football in the background is a bit of a distraction.'

'That's its purpose.'

'A needless distraction.'

'...'

'Murphy?'

'...'

'Cat got your tongue, Murphy?'

'Not at all,' I said, eventually, weak as a kitten.

Stephen looked at me. He'd a glint in his eye, and a healthy sheen on his balding dome. 'Brilliant stuff,' he said, and with that I was done, only my manager, who'd finally discovered a flair for management, was not.

'I'll switch off the screen now,' he said. 'You feel free to finish up the text you were sending and have a packet of Taytos. Oh, and while we're at it, it's probably a good idea that we swap over Buckaroo for Scrabble.'

Murphy Who Talks

In fairness, he was right. I was still yet to get around to that.

Poor Murphy, I replied, to which I received the response *Why?* and I wrote back *Oh, nothing, wrong person*, to which Rebecca wrote *Who were you writing to?* an air of suspicion maybe, or simply an interest as to who I might be mixing her up with.

My mother, I wrote.

I see.

I was eking out undeserved sympathy. Stephen's after turning the football off as no one, bar yours truly, is watching it.

The two-tick grey turned two-tick blue quick fast like, but the response didn't come for a minute or more; an eternity in phoneland. I thought she would tell me my chickens had come home to roost, or query as to whether the talking ban had ever been more, really, than an attempt to watch the football-themed advertising tournament (as she called it), or ask, quite honestly, whether I had considered psychodynamic therapy so as to explore the oedipal mix-up between herself and my dear mother. But no, she responded not with silence, but with the modernity of emoji and two pared back, simple, words.

It's fine xx

I fretted a moment. There were not two words in the English-English language less reassuring than *it's* and *fine* when said or written together.

But Rebecca was not one for passive meaning nor bitten tongues, such that I'd a mind to think it was, on this occasion, fine after all.

It was 21:36.

The warm glow of summer was dead before it had truly begun.

The football tournament I'd longed for would now elude me at least ten percent of the time (which was far too much). I could stream it on the phone, of course, but it wasn't the same. I wanted it there, on the big screen, because it reminded me of the old world, of childhood, while this, the apps and streams, buffering and feeds, this was the new, and I wanted nothing to do with it; a constantly updating life with chaotic unpredictability; the barrage of news and messages or, worse still, nothing at all.

Plus, the big screen was bigger, so it was better, to my magpie-like eyes.

And with that, Stephen switched the telly off at the mains, plunging me into figurative darkness and, briefly, the entire pub too. In his enthusiasm, he'd flipped the bar lights besides.

It was 21:37.

And not only were we now *London's First Silent Pub*, but we were also one of a select few who went against the grain and did not show the football at all.

It was 21:38.

The minutes would drag on endlessly.

'You look like you're going to crap your pants.'

'Right you are, Rebecca.'

'At least put up a mild fight.'

'I was never one to look a fact in the face and call it a liar.'

'What?'

'I agree with you,' I said, went on to say that I had seen myself in the mirror in cobra pose, that it was undeniable I'd the look less of a yogi than I did a toddler engaged in his first conscious shit.

I liked cobra; foreheads on the ground, palms pressed to the mat, pushing our bodies up when Rebecca said 'Lift', as she had twice in class that morning, lightly smiling each time she saw me, in part because it looked as if I were about to shit my shorts, but also because I'd been 'rumbled' as she put it, arguing that my 'mission for peace' had nothing to do with saving the pub from its CPO, or finding inner quiet, more a 'misanthropy' on my part that meant I didn't want to 'face up to' or 'speak with' other people.

And, of course, there was the embarrassment of having texted her, not my mother, by mistake, which she conceded now had seemed a little odd but, as she put it, 'a method of sorts.'

'Right you are, Rebecca,' was all I said, which infuriated her. She grew more amused, more needling, more Donnelly-like in her own way, though as I'd walked myself into trouble by making a monster of Stephen, I had only myself to blame.

'You've dug yourself into a hole, haven't you?' she said, all smirk, as we walked towards the studio before going in separately.

'A little quagmire,' I said, as we passed the Emirates Stadium, itself the victim of a talking ban.

For the uninitiated, that's a football joke, a good one too, promise. Google it up.

Now, later that day, I was in her room; Rebecca instructing me to repeat cobra again, to correct my 'form and posture', the yoga both a useful endeavour, and, like the snake of the same name, a wriggling, meandering distraction from the things she and I wanted to talk about and avoid, respectively.

'Is it not a good thing that I can't imitate a poisonous snake?'

'Not if you look like you're about to shit yourself, it distracts me when I'm teaching my class', she replied.

'Fair enough, so. It would be quite funny if a fella did shit himself in your class though, don't you think?'

'Murder with the hot fans.'

'Curried air.'

'I never needed to hear that sentence,' said Rebecca, to which I hissed like a snake, and she hit me on the nose with a rolled-up copy of *National Geographic Traveller*, a dense and painful magazine.

Frustrated as she was by my evasion, she'd taken pity on me. The Switzerland Serbia game was on in the background, my relief for the day. I lifted myself as Granit Xhaka scored, running to a corner, making a symbol that looked like a homage to *The X Factor* if you didn't know your history, the Albanian flag if you did, or both if you'd Google, had thought first one thing, then the other.

'Would you find it funny if a woman shat herself in class?' said Rebecca.

I watched on, as the Swiss lad celebrated, because he was Swiss, Albanian, both.

'Murphy?'

'Sorry?'

'I asked you if you'd find it funny if a woman crapped herself in my class. Or just farted even?'

A wince, a tired revelation, and the words 'Double standards' escaping from her lips as she read my mind. She was right. Why had *we* a monopoly on the gas craic of scatology?

With tact and indulgence, Rebecca said 'Push your chest out, Murphy, or you'll do your back in.'

She got up off her bed to demonstrate, and perhaps skirt over the things she didn't like about me, in my actions, inactions, words said and, moreover, not.

'Are we going to talk about it, then?' she said, a while later, to which I said 'Now?' and she said 'If not now, when?'.

'Full time?' I said.

'Can this one go to extra time?' she asked and, as it was a group match, I promised her that 'No,' it could not,' not that we spoke of the text after either, Rebecca letting me off with a smile, shook head, and perhaps needing respite from all the talk 'neath the unforgiving heat of the outside and inside air.

'Look,' I said, now, with the game still going on. 'I'm a snake evolving into a lizard.'

I stuck out my tongue like I was hissing and kicked my legs, like they were legs.

'Very nice, Murphy,' said Rebecca, stroking my hair.

Stephen was right about the football. I was the only one who took a blind bit of notice. People came to get away from it. Word of the World Cup Ban had spread fast, across the web.

Where not to watch the World Cup
Places in London to avoid the football
How to avoid the world cup and still go out

The last one pissed me off. Capital letters, lads. Rules are rules.

But Stephen had gone too far. He'd not only banned football, he had also made the pub exclusive, locking the door, installing a scanner that allowed entry upon the scanning of a code found on the pub's newly revamped website. We were no longer a place for waifs and strays.

'It's still free,' he said.
'Is it?'
'Sure, you sign up via email, you get your code.'
'In exchange for data.'
Stephen smiled. 'Exactly.'
'Wonderful.'
I noticed that he was wearing a crisp, new shirt.
'It's quirky,' he said. 'People like quirky.'
'I thought that was the last thing you wanted,' I said, to

which he said 'I never said that,' and I'd to walk away before I fell prey to despair.

The door opened, an unlocking sound. Three men walked inside; from where, I've no clue.

I showed them the menu, another with our rules. They nodded, hinting they'd come for the silence, and knew the score. They chose pints, ticked the Pay-By-Card box and, to my delight, added a pack of Taytos too. I served them two pints of Three and one of Four, and there was a beeping sound off the card machine when one of the lads paid for the round after I'd made an ∞-like symbol with my hands to signal 'together?'.

Other punters looked up.

There was no way around the noise of the card machine.

The boys sat down. The bar was busy. I'd cleaned the shelves, restocked the spirits and wines. We had just two wines now, the choice Red or White. No Rose.

We hadn't the demand for it.

I'd replenished the crisps, cleared glasses, wiped the oaken surface, and was distracted by Mr. Handley, who I'd texted the door code.

He complained about each change, in writing, and I told him (in writing too) change was change and things happened for a reason and we'd to be getting on with it, but he couldn't read my writing and wrote back *just get me a pint Murphy*, to which I added a comma much to my amusement, and his chagrin.

He didn't like the changes, yet came back after each one, and I'd the feeling he had nowhere else to go or better to *be*. I didn't always charge him for his pint, out of pity, and because it went unspoken we'd no charade to go through, and he'd drink it pretending not to be grateful or sad, or sadly grateful,

Murphy Who Talks

and we'd get on with our respective afternoons.

He was there now. He looked up from his *Express* and beckoned me over. Thinking it perfunctory, I wrote down the number he always had on a piece of paper.

Four?

He shook his head, crossed the number out, wrote below.

Five

I wrote, as slow and legibly as I could, and twisted the paper round.

Feeling adventurous are we, Mr. Handley?

He twisted it back.

Shut up, Murphy

I twisted it back to me.

I'm not speaking

Another twist.

You know what I mean

One more.

Right you are

The paper was running out. I went to get the man his drink.

I was shocked. Mr. Handley only drank Four, just the once Three, and that was when I'd forgotten – as per – to tap a keg of the ale that he liked.

Mr. Handley was trying something new.

A beautiful yoga teacher wanted to spend time with me. Stephen had a spine. I'd learned how to talk back to Donnelly. England were playing well.

The world was a scary and exciting place, its constants; Con Connelly, chaos, and the fact that I'd never seen – still haven't – a white person drinking Super Malt, for reasons I don't understand.

Two men came to the bar, one ordered Three, ticking the box. The other?

'Two.'

'Shhhhh!'

It was his friend who said it, and they giggled like rules weren't rules.

Honest to God.

Murphy Who Talks

Chapter Twenty

- *Our noble hero is forced to confront his demons*
- *Panama get a hiding at the hands of Gareth Southgate's red and white army*
- *Rebecca West nudges Murphy towards being an open and honest man*
- *Murphy does a joke to avoid that*
- *Sex and techno*

'You're quieter than usual,' said Rebecca, to which I said, 'No I'm not.'

She smiled. 'Defensive too.'

My back leg was taut, a discomfort shooting up through the hamstring.

I *was* quieter than usual, knew why too, the adult in me smart enough not to admit the child had gotten jealous. I said nothing of it, how I'd looked up in class, watched on as Rebecca pressed her hands into the small of another man's back, correcting his posture; an infantile jealousy in me I was not, it turned out, above feeling. I had it in me, it seemed, the desire to own and be owned, love and be loved, limit and be limited by another.

I lowered my back, smart enough to keep my peace, weak enough to lie.

'Today would have been my dad's birthday,' I said.

This was not a lie, but it was dishonest all the same as, though it was John Snr's birthday, I'd not thought about it until now, when it presented itself as an escape.

With my puerile jealousy I was no better than Donnelly, with my lie, no other man besides. As if reading my thoughts and choosing to entertain my words, Rebecca stood up. She pressed her hands into the small of my back, unknotting me, such that I was able to touch the floor.

'What was it like?' she said.

'What?'

'Growing up without a dad.'

I shrugged.

'Don't shrug, Murphy. You'll put your back out in that position.'

'You can do it if you put your back into it,' I began to sing, only for Rebecca to say 'Now is not the time for Ice Cube'.

'It's very hot,' I said, and she said 'So hot he'd melt', encouraging me to lower my chest to the floor, and turn my head to one side.

'Do I have to answer?'

'Yes,' she said. 'I'd like to know what it was like to lose your dad when you were so little. Growing up. You should tell me. No jokes or tall tales. Just the feelings, and the facts.'

'One?'

'One what?'

'Joke or tale.'

'Okay. One. Then I want to know what it was like for you when you were young.'

So I told her the one about the thing that was brown and sticky, a stick, to which she laughed, and then I told her the one about the dad that went missing, at sea, presumed dead, when I was a young lad.

Murphy Who Talks

I didn't cry, as you don't, not always, with these things, and I did not necessarily see it as cathartic then, as you don't always see it that way at the time. But I did feel better for the honesty of it spoken and open and said and given words, such that I felt I deserved it later when I was held, and she stroked my hair.

At 21:23, according to the alarm clock beside her bed.

These days, Rebecca will occasionally send a meme, taking the Mickey piss out of me, knowing I abhor block capitals. It might be a contrast of yoga and vodka, one a man bending over, the other a lad blackout drunk, the inference being that this is me, having cancelled my membership at The Yoga Studio.

Or she'll send me a picture of a woman with a tight arse, the overlaid, bold white text reading: *Yoga Pants: The Bacon of Clothing*, Rebecca's idiosyncratic way of saying hi, informing me of what I'm missing, her enquiry as to the state of my mind and love life, or a mixture of the above.

Rebecca always follows up with words, a question or two. I respond in kind and, after that, we go on with our respective lives. But before all that, we knew each other once, true and proper, spent time in each other's lives and limbs, in her room, as she never showed any interest in visiting the Lorraine Estate and I hadn't the inclination to invite her, the privacy of that space vital to me the way broken silence was for her, the way being visible was Donnelly, or the routine of work Con.

Nigeria had beaten Iceland.
Costa Rica lost to Brazil.
The Serb lads who'd celebrated with crossed hands were threatened with bans, their gesture deemed political. FIFA didn't do politics. Politics is a threat to profit.
Rebecca, however, did do politics. The talk of it at least.

We had come to an agreement, that if we were not going to talk about what was going on in the country, the whole shebang of it, not knowing whether it was here or there, coming or going, in or out, then we'd to speak with frank honesty about a topic of Rebecca's choosing, my parents not off-limits, a bit off-limits, mostly off-limits overall.

It was either that, or we talk about Brexit, so went the agreement. I was not, I said, inclined to discuss the latter with someone who had voted the same way as me.

'Do you get on with your siblings?' she asked, an hour or so after Costa Rica had lost to Brazil.

'Well enough,' I said. 'Eileen Jnr. sends pics of the kids and updates of her legal situation, Little John analyses risks for a large construction firm in Dublin.'

'Legal situation?'

'She's in a dispute with her work.'

'Ah. And John Jnr. What are the risks he looks at?'

'They were low, they are now high, with easterly gales,' I said, and Rebecca uttered the ineffable B word, to which I said, 'Yes' adding that he 'sends pictures of his cats too'.

For a moment there was the closest thing to silence we ever had in Rebecca's room.

I looked at the fan, remembered the whirring noise of my nebuliser as a child, sitting next to my older brother with the telly on, he a Maverick to my Goose, and told Rebecca 'I'll be seeing him later in the summer,' to which she said, 'Well that's good. Is he coming over?'

'No,' I said. 'We're doing a pilgrimage home.'

'You and your brother?'

'No, Donnelly and Con. My brother's already there.'

'Of course. Why are you going to Ireland?'

'The weather,' I said, to which Rebecca stuck out her

tongue, and I flirted with saying you could come but chose not to ruin it.

Rebecca lit up a fag, exhaled into the afternoon air. 'That'll be good for you,' she said.

'It's always nice going home.'

Rebecca laughed.

'This is your home, Murphy. The King of Holloway.'

She laughed again, when I began to pout.

I told her I was a republican, and was all set to elaborate, only for Rebecca to say 'Cool, couldn't care less,' asking me instead to describe the scenery in Ireland. So I did, at length.

It was midafternoon.

We served each other's needs well. Rebecca stole me from loneliness, self-loathing, memory and thought. I blocked out the silence, filling her room with a curious mix of the trivial, the sexual, the honest and the absurd and, on that front, I was the tonic she needed to get through that summer's heatwave, the one in the air, in the papers, on the news, in her family, in the body and the mind.

Tunisia got a hiding off Belgium.

The Koreans fell short against Mexico.

Germany saved their skins by getting one over Sweden, on a green field in Sochi, a 95th minute free kick which, if you were a Swede, likely seemed a bad joke.

As a clown, I loved them for it.

A clown is a jester with furrows and colour, flirting with giving up, punch-drunk on love and hope.

A clown without hope is a headstone.

I'd high hopes for The Purser's Retainer. Of all the things Rebecca told me I hid (and she was right), it's important to note that I wasn't solely trying to seek distraction or avoid human interaction (though these things are also true).

I truly did believe it was funny to create *London's First Silent Pub*, and if I were being honest, I'd have to admit the way the joke boomeranged on me was likely the funniest thing at all.

That, or the day we hosted Alcoholic's Anonymous for a local mime artist troupe.

Yes, I'd my silent pub and Cyrillic menus, my charity, my desire to get one over London and all its injustices if only I saved the pub, saw it through the summer, that lean time of year when the happy people are out and about at barbecues and in parks, at festivals and on holidays; summer, that mirror of a season, holding up to you the realities of loneliness, detachment and, in some cases, despair.

Yes, we served each other's needs well.

After sex, I would punctuate the silent air with a 'honk honk' or 'hu hu' or a 'bongo!' to ease the tension, the pair of us ignoring my desperation to grow closer to her, and her inability to allow that, with its dangerous permanency.

Rebecca dictated the terms.

When she wanted distraction from silence and thought she would have me drone on, listening to me like I was music. When she wanted frank honesty, she'd prod me. It pleased her if I was honest, pleased her still if she felt she'd moved me – even if only in increments – towards being honest with myself. And if I veered away from talking with and to her about it all Rebecca, for the most part, humoured me, knowing as she did the limits I had within myself to be frank and honest about it all.

I would recount the likes of Devonde Memphis from the Sea Bass farm in Ostend; Ted Wellings, who broke his leg mountain climbing in Denmark the year we were sherpas in Jutland, and of course, my dear old friend Hugh Briss, to evade, but to amuse myself also and, most importantly, her, the look of amusement on a woman's face the sweetest thing there ever was.

'Hugh Briss?'

'Yes,' I said. 'Jewish lad I worked with at a café in Harrow. Nice fella, touch arrogant. Got fired for excessive posturing.'

'You're a clown, Murphy,' she would say, and I'd say 'Aye', and we would talk on.

She would prod, and at times I would reveal, or Freudian slip my way into revelation, an unconscious part of me grateful to her for the prodding I kidded myself into believing I wished to evade.

'Tell me more about the breakdown,' she said one afternoon, as I stretched on her floor. Inhaling, and without thinking, I said, 'Which one?', exhaled, and froze.

Rebecca, laying on her bed, looked me square in the face, raising her eyebrows.

'The one you wrote the article about,' she said, to which I said 'Ah' and before the spoken equivalent of a two-tick grey'd gone blue was met with 'There was another one?', to which I said 'Plural' without thinking.

Adult conversation, by way of baby steps.

Rebecca leant up, covering one breast with her white linen sheet. A cliché. This is a novel. She leaned over, picked up her cigarettes, and said, 'Do go on'.

So I told her about the first time I'd had 'sweating eyes', about therapy, about connecting dots with that and this and this and that; namely John, how losing a father at four did indeed leave a mark.

And I told her about the breakdown a couple of years earlier, when I'd cried at work, between Printer 1 and Gillian Barker's desk, and was taken into a separate room (with glass walls) to explain why I was a thirty-year-old man crying in an office half my age.

'There is a strong case for the return of the cubicle to the workplace,' I said.

'It would be a regressive step, I think.'

'Probably, I replied.'

In Rebecca's room I struck poses; physical and other, but she did tease out the honesty.

'We're not so different,' she said, the afternoon when Senegal drew with Japan.

I disagreed. I reminded her of the things she believed in; the value of protest, why it was important to 'take a side', that kale had taste, beetroot crisps too.

She smiled.

'Yes, but I admit there are things that bother me. That eat away at me.'

'Like a caterpillar.'

'I rest my case.'

She sat up. 'Don't you ever feel angry about it all? The way the world's going?'

'I do. I am,' I said, said too that I was angry as hell most if not all of the time, as Lo-Fi techno played on her laptop in the background, gently.

I said I was angry as hell with all the twisted words and wilful lies. I told Rebecca that if this was what they were going to do with 'words' and how they were going to treat 'my people', that is, not Czechs nor Irish or English but just the 'decent and occasionally indecent among us', then yes, I was angry.

If they were to take the things we loved, values valued and twist the words I saw as sacred I was going to act the fool, onwards. They'd made a fool of the world, so what was the point in dignifying it with anything other than foolishness?

'You're a cynic,' she said. 'So that you don't have to deal with it all.'

Murphy Who Talks

I shrugged.

'Rebecca, there's truths I'd rather not face, the same way there's truths you'd not either. If I don't laugh about the mess of it all, I'll give up hope. If I don't laugh at it, it's like giving in. Laughter is just anger with better PR.'

She nodded.

'You were looking me in the eye saying that.'

'I was.'

'Will we ever talk about it all?'

'We will.'

'But not today?'

'It's too warm.'

'Tomorrow will be the same.'

'It'll be the August Bank Holiday before you know it,' I said. 'That's always a rainy day.'

She smiled. 'Okay. Deal.'

She beckoned me towards her. I shuffled across the bed – like a caterpillar – and things happened, things that can be beautiful between humans, and the complexities in humans they stir. I for one lost track of time.

England beat Panama by six goals to one.

Chapter Twenty-One

- *Murphy reflects*
- *The FIFA World Cup chunters on*
- *Stephen goes mad with power, and does a joke*
- *Murphy assesses the importance of male friendship*

Colombia thumped the Poles, Uruguay the Russians, and the Saudis beat the Egyptians while Iran, Portugal, Spain and Morocco all drew, not with each other. That would be absurd. It is a game of two sides, as halves.

The pub ticked by. It was quiet in the daytimes but not as quiet as you'd expect a pub to be, busier than most even. Stephen had introduced Wednesday Whiskey Tasting and Tuesday Gin Nights and The Thursday Night Quiz, which was of course silent, so it essentially felt like sitting a GCSE exam.

He was loving it.

Indeed, when I was there, I often saw him sipping a whiskey or gin, appreciating it in studied silence, noting down his thoughts so he could share them with a punter or two. He might be seen doing his *Guardian* crossword, reading a book, or sitting in pensive, reflective thought. It was everything I'd ever wanted, assuming, that is, I have been honest about my intentions this entire time.

Murphy Who Talks

The Danes and French drew in a war of attrition. Argentina saved their Danish bacon in the last minutes against Nigeria. Croatia beat Iceland, so the latter went back to their wealthy, beautiful, chilly land. The Koreans shocked the Germans, and the Germans too went home.

Brazil beat the Serbs and the Swiss and Costa Ricans drew, and it was a Tuesday and hot as hell like every day that month, and I'd gotten a text off Connelly which said *Are working this evening?*, to which I'd written back *I am ConBoy, yes* and he wrote *you're working like a dog boyo good stuff!*

I thanked the gods of Catholic ardour that had Con think working all hours was a good way to shape one's life.

We liked each other a great deal, me and Rebecca. But we didn't agree on all matters; didn't agree that calling Donald Trump a racist on Twitter was pointless (my view), that wearing blue face paint with yellow stars at a march in London had purpose (hers), or that people who chose *this* might also be *that*, that *this* meant you were a certain sort of person in totality not some muddled mix of good, bad, both.

Her internal world, of such nuanced complexity, meant she'd to make the external black and white. I was inclined to think it, we, were more complicated than that.

'Pffft,' was her reply, upon my mooting this notion. 'Sometimes there's right, and sometimes there's wrong.'

Fingers interlocked, I stretched towards the ceiling.

'If we had eggs and bacon we could have bacon and eggs if we only had the bacon,' I said.

Rebecca looked at me, up and down. 'Shut up, Murphy.'

I released my stretch and bent towards the floor.

'Grand so.'

I placed my hands behind my ankles, and pulled up,

stretching my hamstrings, glad one of us, at least, was becoming more flexible. I stared at the wooden floor, as my hamstrings cried out for a rest.

'There have to be times when you want to scream about all the madness that's going on in the world,' said Rebecca, returning to that conversation of a few days earlier, dissatisfied with what I had said, needing me to give her more on the matter, or simply admit I was wrong and that I agreed with her.

I noticed a fleck of white paint on the floor, from decorating way back when.

'All the time,' I said. 'I just don't get angry about it the same way as you. Anger bores me.'

She said 'pffft' again.

I told her I was bored of those angry who hadn't been before all this, those raging mad such that they wanted us to lose the run of ourselves, and go fully insane, bored of people saying it had nothing to do with Karolina's lot, when it did, and bored of hearing about a history that never existed, so bored I couldn't be angry about it anymore.

She sniffed the air, derisively.

'I think that's sad.'

I released my palms from behind my heels.

'It is,' I said. 'And I am. Compared to sadness, anger is a cakewalk, Rebecca.'

She said 'pffft' once more, with less force.

'Says the man who refuses to confront his own.'

'Eh?'

'Sadness.'

I smiled. 'Ah. I never said I was no hypocrite, Rebecca.'

She nodded, dare I say appreciatively, and reminded me that though it was still June, 'the August Bank Holiday' was 'just around the corner,' to which I said 'I know.'

She stretched out an arm, compelling me to her side of the

Murphy Who Talks

room.

Colombia beat Senegal, the Poles did one over Japan.

It was a curious one, that summer. In discord, I discovered a measure of harmony, not least in the things I was forced to confront in Rebecca's room, where I would play and joke, yes, but stretch, reveal, be prodded, and reveal a little more.

We agreed the Internet was 'mad altogether', my words, not hers, and agreed it was worse for women despite our male delusion that attention was always good.

'You learn to suspect the worst with DM requests,' said Rebecca. 'It shouldn't be that way.'

She told me that the threats were the worst, then the sense, life-learned, that you'd brought it upon yourself. She said the dick pics were horrifying and that, if you were lucky enough not to suffer those, the shallow nature of the space in general was pretty horrific as well. As such, she used the apps and Internet as little as she could, which 'was just about fine' for a yoga teacher if 'not ideal'.

She still used Instagram, sparingly, and WhatsApp most often, but not Twitter, as she had in her 'marketing years', for it was 'toxic'.

'And an echo chamber,' I said, to which she replied, 'There's worse things than an echo chamber, Murphy' and I asked 'How so?'

'Being called a thick libtard slut springs to mind.

I nodded.

She nodded back.

'Silly me,' I said.

'Silly you,' she said, and on we moved.

Rebecca's relationship with the Internet meant relationships had wilted over the years, and it was here that we differed most. People had gradually slipped from her life, and she let it happen, with neither regret nor disregard. People were busy, with lives to live, mortgages to pay, weddings to attend, kids to have and raise. Others, it was clear to Rebecca, were simply happy to let life pass by, a friendship not vital if it slipped over time. She was okay with this, it was the way it was, and she took the hint of radio silence to be a hint of life moving from one phase to another.

'You're not made up that way,' she said. 'Are you?'

'Not particularly,' I said, my hands wrapped around my ankles, knees and head protectively buried in the floor. 'One likes to be adored.'

She smiled.

'Tell me about Karolina.'

It threw me, but I did. I told her of the red hair, green eyes, those loving eyes, and finally, mutually sweating eyes, when something, call it homesickness, economics, nostalgia, family or language, and the illusion of being understood, had drawn me home.

'Towards the end *there*,' I said. 'I began to think of *here* as different to what I'd left behind. You head out with small plans and big hopes. The years float by, you begin to wonder if the place you left behind is so bad after all. I loved Karolina more than life itself, but something still drew me home. Home, I'd say.'

Rebecca was upside down in my vision, as I'd my head still to the mat on the floor.

'You're weeping,' she said.

'No, I've just got sweaty eyes,' I said, and with pity, she had a nice little giggle at that.

'I was in a rut. I'd a low spell, again, and convinced myself that England was quite *nice*.'

'And?'

'It is. It isn't. It's both. Either way, within six months I was home, having got a full head of madness.'

I told Rebecca then that I'd to live with my decision, to leave Prague, Karolina, a life, behind. I told her about the hottish summer of 2014, the closest I ever felt 'to being English', when I was homesick, such that England became a symbol of hope and opportunity.

'And look what I came back to,' I said, said too 'But that was my fault. It was already here.'

I lifted my head from the mat, stretched my back, and looked at Rebecca.

'Do you miss her?

I thought of lying, thought too that was the last thing Rebecca would want.

'Aye.'

The clock read 23:33.

England lost to Belgium and came second in their group. Panama lost to Tunisia. They came last. The revolution had been publicised not televised, was popular and so normalised to the point that it was no revolution at all.

We were increasingly homogenous in our demographic; young, white, male, mostly middle class I'd say, from the way they carried themselves, the books they read, the craft beers ordered with a written 3 or 8 or 11 on the menu, me as capable as any other in identifying a fella as this or that because he read that book or wore this brand.

The only thing they didn't do was speak. It was just as well. I'd enough of my presumptive and judging mind.

The national mood was, undeniably, better, the World Cup a salve to the unrelenting, harsh reality of the news. And if supporting England meant that, so be it; if supporting England meant not being full Irish, half Irish or Irish at all, I was willing to play along, if only so people were nicer to one another for a few days.

We were distracted, and it was beautiful.

We were laughing, and that was beautiful too.

Football was an escape. The Purser's Retainer was an escape. *London's First Silent Pub* was an escape, if not the one I'd hoped for.

Yoga was an escape. Friendships were not meant to be an escape but they were, and I was in danger of letting mine slide, such that I'd to ask myself if I was a true friend, given I'd disappeared at the first sign of hope, love, distraction or whatever it was that drew me to Rebecca's room.

In the morning I did the line clean. We did it Mondays, and today wasn't Monday, but everything was upside down so why not do it on another day altogether?

A line clean is a mechanical and satisfying endeavour. You turn off the gas. You hook the barrel nozzles up to these little holes that look like gas masks in the cellar wall, and you rid the pressure pumps of any liquid, then the taps too. Then you fill a giant vat of water and you hook that to the lines, and feed water through them like an IV drip. It's a satisfying endeavour, lengthy too, giving you time to think about it all, or if you want to avoid that, dick around on your phone.

Have you ever thought of writing a letter? my favourite yoga teacher wrote to me, to which I wrote back *No, unless it's one of complaint.*

My friend Lydia lost her father when she was eleven, and said she found it cathartic.

My thumb hovered over the green keyboard. I'd a joke about my old friend Cath Arctic, and a serious point to make about letters to dead people, but didn't press the pad, hovering instead.

MURPHY WHO TALKS

Water spattered from the Heineken tap, telling me the line was clear, ready to be cleaned. I lowered my thumb, but before I could reply, Rebecca had written to me again.

It's just an idea. I'll stop. Not my place to prod xx

I went about my work.

I fed chemicals that are good for pipes but not people into the pipes that give liquid to them, and came within a whisker of writing don't, I need you, but instead sent a facetious gif Rebecca's way, and was responded to with one of her own, tact a virtue she had on her part the way I'd a hypocritical aversion for the words I loved when it came to hard truths, cruel blows, the things that hurt and dead parents.

I did the line clean. We opened the pub. Customers came in and ordered pints of Six and Three, Two and Four.

No one argued.

But in not arguing, no one talked to, or with, each other. No one agreed or disagreed or talked 'til they'd found somewhere in between, and everyone sat in front of me appeared the same but for the presumptions I had of them, from the way they looked based on clothes, age, haircut, skin colour and, in Mr. Handley's case, newspaper preference.

In The Purser's Retainer, I'd created an infantile illusion of equality, shorn of the difficult and beautiful bit of life; the words.

I tend to go for a run these days, if I'm getting up and about, or I use my gym membership. I seldom do yoga, haven't the time.

But every so often, I will, to remind myself of that summer, or simply check in on my flexibility; repeating those movements I learned first at the studio and then in her room, as she laughed, and criticised, encouraged, mocked and helped.

I'll separate my feet, turn towards a wall, or put head to

knee, gauging whether the tug in my hamstrings is the same as before, to see if anything's changed, to see if anything ever changes, or if it's just a waste of time and we were right to be cynical after all.

Usually, I conclude we'd reason, yet were not right all the same. It explained but didn't excuse, and as such I promise myself I'll give the yoga another go one day, if only to believe, as I came dangerously close to believing in the hot, scary, sweaty summer of 2018.

Stephen had given me the night off.

No, he'd foisted the night off upon me.

'I'll keep things ticking over here, Murphy. You know I've always been a rugby man. That reminds me of Benny Galatasaray.'

'Who's he?'

'A guy who played hooker when the two of us were at school. Nice guy. Loose morals.'

'...'

'That was a joke, Murphy.'

'I know,' I said.

It was 12:06.

I worked 'til 16:00, was meant to be on 'til 18:00, only for Stephen to say those words 'I'll keep things ticking over here.'

The joke? No, it wasn't the hooker line, though I'd to admit I did like it. The joke was that I was relieved. I wanted to see England play. The childish FOMO that'd seen me through life with three breakdowns, a chip on my shoulder, a runner of a mouth and a face-saving inability to argue, handle conflict or take anything seriously at all had reared its ugly head.

Now, it was England I wanted in on, the England that represented everything I sorely didn't want to see, feel or be, but kind of did.

I wanted to watch the game, as did Donnelly and Con, so we arranged to watch it in Erin's Rejoinder, less to dilute the red- and white-flagged elements of it, more for the guarantee of a seat.

I knew that they would question me as to why I'd been missing in recent weeks, knew also I'd to ask myself why, when I valued loyalty, honesty and whatever in the name of God fraternity was, I'd taken to secrets, lying and evasion of an altogether different kind than I was used to.

But I was going to make it up to them, with my presence, if nothing else, and I went there in good time.

And it was 17:56.

And there was just an hour before the game.

Chapter Twenty-Two

- *Our noble hero goes to The Regional Pickpocket*
- *Face-paint fun*
- *Ryanair's 'enjoyable' new baggage policies come under scrutiny*
- *England win a penalty shootout, for the sake of all that is glorious fuck*

You couldn't make head nor tail of it. At the end of the night, you couldn't tell if I was this or that, that or this.

So here's what happened.

It was the night of jerk colcannon and curried soda bread, Ackee n' Guinness, barmbrack if you were feeling prudish, rum cake if you'd a kick-in-your cake sort of need.

A Jamaican born lad was playing and a lad whose dad was Jamaican born was playing and a lad whose granddad the same, and there were a couple of boys like me who were Irish, not full Irish (the three lions on the shirt was a giveaway) or maybe, to their mind, not really Irish at all.

It was none of my damn business.

Sadly for the Jamaican, not Jamaican, a bit Jamaican lads, the country didn't share my view.

Murphy Who Talks

I'd a plaintive air about myself. The roar and talk and noise of The Regional Pickpocket was at odds with the silence I'd sought, attained and squandered, and I was enjoying it.

After dithering, we'd decided to watch it in The Regional Pickpocket, not Erin's Rejoinder, after all. The young were there, by proxy hope and life too. I was enjoying it.

I was also dressed as a clown.

I still told myself I'd no love for the country in which I'd been born. But I loved the innards of it, some of it at least, loved how this spoiled city of mine, 'neath its Grayling Estates and litter and supermarkets filled with that and this, this and that, was by and large good. And I loved that it was lads from cities like mine who were there dicking around on a green rectangle in Russia. And here the three of us were, myself, Con boy, and Donnelly; pint men extraordinaire.

We had, the each of us, left something of ourselves behind; Con Connelly his aversion to booking tables (we'd a decent spot near a corner, near the bar). Donnelly his aversion to other human beings, and me my aversion to England, noise, and pale ale, which I'd a pint of now.

It wasn't so bad.

A young woman with a Jheri curl and an England top had turned to face us in a manner that would have given advertisers the horn, Nigel Farage bad dreams. She'd a St. George flag on her face.

'You boys want yours done?' she said, pointing to our faces with her pencil, easel and sponge.

Donnelly said yes. Connelly too. Me yes, but no, but yes also.

'He does this,' Connelly said, when the girl looked confused.

Call it loyalty, principle, denial or childishness, I fought joining in only to be told 'You're joining in', only to say 'But can you do me a Georgian flag?' as I'd 'a thing for their wine'.

'He does this,' said Con. 'Ignore him.'

'He's a moron,' said Donnelly.

'What's your name, little fella?' the woman said.

'Murphy.'

'Just Murphy?'

'Fact-o.'

'How lovely.'

'Meh.'

'I only have red and white paint,' she said, and I said 'Them's the colour of Georgia's flag', to which she said 'Well I don't know what it looks like, but if you fancy, I can paint you like a clown.'

It was the first time in a while me, Con Connelly and Declan Donnelly had nodded our heads in agreement, suggesting that was a smart thing to do.

So she did.

There I was, watching England, dolled up to look like The Joker. The game began.

A lad with a dad from Nigeria passed the ball to the one with an Irish gran.

France had won, Uruguay too.

Russia shocked the Spanish and the Croats beat the Danes; penalties both times, and it was cruel if you happened to be from Denmark or Spain. Football is an inherently cruel game.

Mexico lost to Brazil as Mexico always do, and Belgium beat Japan and I later found out via Googling that they had won twice and drawn twice and, now with the latest edition, lost twice when playing Belgium.

I liked that.

Sweden had beaten the Swiss, in the Battle of the Neutral Nations, or the Battle of Nations Starting with the Letters S

Murphy Who Talks

and W.

And now I was watching England play Colombia with a Dutch beer in my hand, Irish teeth my mouth, English fags my pocket, a Bic lighter from where I do not know.

'You're very quiet, Murphy,' said Donnelly, to which I said 'Not at all' and he said 'That's the first thing you've said in ten minutes' and to be honest with you it was.

I'm glad you talked to me about her. Talking's healthy Murphs, done the right way ;) xx

I sent her a selfie, an *I know*, and a smiley emoji face besides.

'Rules are rules, Donnelly,' I said. 'And I know you like to concentrate during a game, so I thought I'd keep quiet,' I said, to which Donnelly said 'You've never kept quiet before'.

You look like Ronald McDonald, she wrote, to which Donnelly nodded at my phone and said, with his inimitable smirk 'What's his name?'

I'll see you tonight, after the football?

I smiled, resigned to who the pair of us were.

'Eduardo Van Der Listicle,' I said, to which he said 'Seriously, who you talking to?' and I said 'I'm only sorting out the crisp order with Stephen, no scandal to report' and he fell quiet a moment, and I wrote back *Indeedio* and *xxx* with smiley emoji face of my own besides.

The game ticked on.

'Send me your passport details,' said Donnelly, minutes later. 'I need to do the online check-in this week.'

I took a sip.

'Will do,' I said, and Donnelly said 'You too, Con,' and he said he would and we sipped on as England played on and I realised I'd completely forgotten it was Don who had booked the flights months earlier, for a week hence, to Ireland, the three of us FOMO incarnate if England were to win the game, and the next one, as we'd be over *there* then, wishing we were *here* with, I don't know, our people?

I'd no idea, knew only that it always seemed I was out of town or place or sorts at the wrongest times, just as I was now in luck for a change.

'Another round?' said Con.

'Sure.'

'To be sure?' he said, needling, jostling County *Kark* voice on him.

'Sure.'

He went to get the round.

None of us were bad people, or had (wholly) or were bad characters, in the literary sense, though we gave a good impression of it, with our supposed lack of conflict, between us, within us. We lived, like most men, surface-level lives.

The thing I liked about the pair of them, and the trio of us, was the fact we'd nothing and everything in common, often agreed on little, often agreed on much.

I couldn't stomach Donnelly's outlook, he hadn't the patience or inclination to consider mine, and I wasn't usually strong enough to say *come on now* or *you're wrong Don* or – and it'd only happened a few times – rile him up something fierce by calling him Declan, which he abhorred.

In doing so, I *triggered* him, stooping to his level, for in doing so I was not convincing, changing or reasoning with him, no, I was solely eking out the pleasure of being the irritant when too inarticulate to win the argument, too insecure to call him out on those occasions when I knew he was wrong, that a woman had a vagina not a cunt, that she was a woman, not a cunt and tits, that I did not want to 'present the very best of myself' on the dating apps because then how would she be able to stomach the foibles and vulnerabilities and

Murphy Who Talks

shortcomings that came off me like steam from an iron?

I was shy.

I was insecure.

I could, though you mightn't believe it, be quiet.

I could be jealous.

I was bad at lists. And similes besides.

I didn't even speak in my own accent, such was the lifelong unease with which I'd carried myself, and the way I chased after something lost and gone.

As for myself and Con, we agreed on most things cultural, political, social and musical, and that which we didn't we put to one side and spoke only of those things that we did.

I didn't agree with every word that came from Con's mouth, nor the context or ingredients of some words he used, but again it was for the tripartite reasoning that I wanted an easy life, was not strong enough to critique his own and, by and large, was willing to sit in silence, watching or sipping with him just the same way he was me.

So no, we were not fine literary characters if it was chaos and conflict you were after. Conflict was to be found on the inside of us, in the silent and unsaid. Me and my search for meaning, distraction, craic and peace, an unobtainable quartet at the best of times. Connelly his loss of Daisy, who he'd the knowing inside himself that he yearned for still, yet yearned a little in himself to accept it was the loss not the woman for whom he yearned, the certainty of the before glossing over the things that caused the now to be the after.

And Donnelly?

Well, Donnelly was a borderline sociopath.

But for all our disagreements over that and this and this and that, it was as easy to sit and listen to Donnelly waffle on about what was wrong with me as it was for us to sit without a word, sipping our pints.

The joke, the real joke, was that if England did get beyond the last sixteen, the one time I actually felt a bit of something for it (I won't say pride), I would not be there.

I'd be *home*, as it were.

And here I was, presuming the English would reach not only the next round but the one after that. Presumptuous. I was more English than I realised.

They scored a penalty goal. There were hugs. With strangers, between the strange mongrel trio that was ourselves, of Scot and rose, lion and shamrock.

I see the man with the large chin scored, said Rebecca, in a moment between the moments, when neither Con nor Don seemed to take much notice.

He did so, I wrote, to which Rebecca replied *are you glad* and I replied *yes of course of course I wouldn't be that petty*, and she said *yeah, but are you happy to see England winning?*

I answered honestly. Asked her how the classes she'd taught thus far today had gone.

Hot, sweaty, largely empty, wrote Rebecca, the one-tick grey going nigh on straight to two-tick blue when Con noted my finger-tapping distraction and said 'Who's that Murphy?'

I thought quick as a flash, said 'John Jnr, he wants to know if we're driving', and as Donnelly couldn't and Connelly and myself wouldn't (we'd plans to enjoy ourselves) I wrote back *no, we're not driving.*

What? wrote Rebecca.

Ah, I wrote, *wrong thread, was writing to my brother about Ireland.*

Please can you stop mixing up members of your family with the woman you're sleeping with she wrote, a smiley face emoji to take the edge off, and I promised I'd try.

Con dropped the subject.

Murphy Who Talks

The game continued. England nearly scored again. And again. And again. But they didn't.

So at the very end Colombia scored, which meant extra time, and Donnelly said 'I'll get a round in before they (pointing to the students) go to the bar', and he did.

You could have a Nigerian dad or Irish mam or Indian grandparents or Bangladeshi father and mother or none of those at all, for if you'd taken a jot of interest in that pointless wonderful game, and had grown up in England, you'd have seen them teeter towards the terror of penalties what seemed like a hundred times or more.

I was desperate that it not go to penalties; for England, so I could go see Rebecca. Which, I was unsure.

I'd seen England win a penalty shoot-out just one other time; against Spain, at Euro '96, the final whistle blowing as Mum informed me, my sister and Little John too that we'd to go to Saturday evening Mass.

'*Please* can we watch the penalties?' my brother asked.

'How long do they last?'

'Depends.'

'How long can it last?'

'Two minutes?' he said, a question, such that Mum said 'That means ten', but let us watch all the same, and England won.

That was 1996. This was 2018.

Much had changed.

I had pubic hair, student debt, and a repeat prescription of Fluoxetine. Wimpy had gone out of, then back into, business.

England won the penalties.

And when it came to it, a lad from Gloucester who grew up in Portugal scored the kick that won the game.

What a world.

I think you're smitten, Murphy Rebecca wrote to me, after I'd written to her, unprompted.

YES!!!!!

As for our faces, you couldn't tell if they had been England or Georgia, or if we were clowns; happy, sad, relieved, with sweating eyes, or a mix of them all.

It was 22:03.

'...'
  '...'
    '...'
  '...'
'...'

She'd lovely eyes Rebecca. I told her that.

'...'
'...'

After the game there had been beeping cars and loud foghorns and *jewels remain* and the odd god-awful rendition of 'England Til I Die', though for once I didn't feel the needle of it, for there was, above all else, a joy in the air, devoid of the usual menace.

'...'
'...'

There was saying *it's coming home* to strangers, which Con did, and Don did and maybe (I can't remember) I did too.

'...'
'...'

And then I was at Rebecca's. She laughed when I said 'Can I have some toast please?', laughed silly as she made sobering tea and toast with a hint of honey while I washed off the make-up, when her housemate walked in, screamed, ran out, and I'd to apologise for 'scaring the fuck out of me' and 'getting red and white face paint all over the sink.'

Murphy Who Talks

I drank my tea. Ate my toast, got remnants of face paint on Rebecca's lips and cheeks and breasts and other places besides, then lay in silence and ellipses, looking at her in the dark of night, the sound one of a country celebrating, not at war with itself for once. That was the sound that came to us from out in the street.

For once, Rebecca seemed content with the silence within her room too, 'til she asked me to repeat exactly what her housemate had said, so I did, and the pair of us had a giggle at that, then went to sleep, at around 00:06, I'd say.

Chapter Twenty-Three

- *The World Cup has a hiatus*
- *Murphy tries to recognise Pride so that his business is not out of touch*
- *Visits Benny Stobart-Peston*
- *Sailor Jerry Bundt cake*

They, we, I'd…

Even now I'm unsure which I was, in or out, part of it all, above it all, beneath it all, included or excluded. Whatever the answer, we shared one common bond.

Black, white, Asian, we were all cloying 'neath the hottest summer any of us could recall. Fanning yourself on the train was now a natural action, all the words in the freebie mags and papers finding meaning, finally, as paper fans that offered respite from the hot, still air. Without the distraction of the games there was no distraction from the heat, though the heat itself served a purpose, binding the nation together in suffering, helping us ignore the news.

So there was that to thank it for.

Rebecca's classes were largely empty, but she still had to turn up for work, even as people avoided Bikram in their droves, the notion of stretching in forty-degree heat repelling

Murphy Who Talks

most. The pub still drew numbers, though not as many as before. Stephen was in denial, saying that we were 'ticking along absolutely nicely', such that I concluded he'd lost his mind.

'Stephen, you know I'm in Ireland next week,' I said, to which he said 'A raging hooligan, a done-gone fool', which made no sense.

'Stephen I've to go to Ireland, I won't be here all week.'

'Brilliant stuff,' he said, and I went back into the bar and wrote a note on a napkin to Mr. Handley who, for all his flaws, had remained loyal to the pub despite its changes.

Mr. Handley, if Stephen asks where I am next week, can you tell him I'm in Ireland?

He simply nodded. I think he knew Stephen had gone mad.

I looked around. It was a Wednesday, there were ten or so heads in the pub. Yes, we were nicely 'ticking by'. But we needed to do more, to try something new to make the most of the summer, now in full flow. And it occurred to me that the coming Saturday, the last shift I had before going away with Donnelly and Con, was Pride. This was a business. And Pride was *business*.

We'd to look like we cared about it all, regardless of whether or not we did. We'd to recognise Pride to keep the gods of front line marketing happy.

I went to visit Mr. Stobart-Peston.

'Stephen, will you watch the bar an hour, I've to go get us some supplies for Pride,' I said, whispering quietly in the back room, where he was eating a pack of Taytos, and dicking around on his phone.

'Grand so,' I think he said, betwixt a mouthful of Cheese & Onion crisps.

My dye guy was a man named Benny Stobart-Peston, an

Antiguan lad who'd moved to the UK in 1963, worked as a road sweeper, signal operator, traffic warden and shit stirrer, saving enough money to open his own store midway up the Seven Sisters Road, which sold this and that, that and this; food dyes, innatural paints, wicker shit, and everything in between.

The last time I saw Benny, Antigua had been taking in migrants from Barbuda, its closest neighbour, recently pummelled by Storm Maria.

Now, I asked him how things were going with the clean-up and rebuild in the towns and cities, mountain villages and tiny hamlets, resorts and hotels.

Bad, bad, bad, bad, fantastic and fabulous was more or less his summary of that.

By and large, Antigua had been bruised not battered, and Benny was grateful to the Lord.

'We have only Him above to thank,' he said.

'A hundred percent true Benny,' I replied. 'The Lord is our guide and shepherd. Our merciful lodestar. Who are we to qu–'

'Cut the shit, Murphy,' said Benny.

So I did. He knew full well my thoughts on Him above.

Him above could have stopped the storm below, had he wanted.

'Alright, okay, fine, good good,' I said. 'How's business?'

'Ticking by.'

'Brilliant stuff,' I said, and, sensing Benny was in no mood for shit-shooting, added 'Enough foreplay. I'm here for supplies, Benny.'

'BB pellets?'

'No, that cat's not been seen in weeks. New home, dead, chasing squirrels in the park, either way, he's no bother to me now.'

Murphy Who Talks

'Silent socks?'

'They were no good at all, Benny. Juliette could still hear me knocking about the place.'

'A bad workman–'

'I wasn't blaming you,' I said. 'It was the bull, not the china shop, if you catch my drift.'

'Fine. What is it that you need, Murphy?'

'Food dyes.'

'You baking again?' he said, an air of not unwarranted excitement to him; he'd tried my Sailor Jerry Bundt cake.

I shook my head. 'No, I've no time for baking these days. Too much work.'

He shook his own.

'I don't have dyes, Murphy. Sorry.'

I was shocked. Benny always had dyes.

'A nightmare, Benny,' I said, telling him he was the 'only fella in town' who'd indigo and violet along with the usual suspects. 'And you know I'm a fucker for honesty.'

He raised his hands in the air.

'I know, Murphy, I know. But what can I do? They sell like... Bundt cakes.'

It was appreciated.

'However so?' I said, recalling how the last time I'd needed indigo and violet food dye (a Deep Purple birthday cake for my friend Jenny Memphis) he'd been my Lord, saviour and, even if the dyes themselves were nine months out of date, saving grace.

'Pride,' he said, views clothed thinly, 'neath a businesslike sneer. 'They all at it.'

He explained how word had got out that he sold the spectrum of the rainbow, in food-dye form, and with Pride around the corner men, women and 'them in-betweens' came in droves.

'Steady on, Benny,' I said. 'In-betweens is a little mean, I'd say, wouldn't yo–'

Benny cut me off, and said he'd sold out of dye, what with people needing it for charity fun runs, office bake sales, and other such events.

I nodded. Uncomfortably, cravenly perhaps, I moved the conversation along. 'A disaster,' I said. 'Well, never mind. I'll think of another way to mark Pride at the pub.'

His shop bell rang. A customer walked in, and straight to the reusable hat racks.

'You up at The Purser's Retainer now?' said Benny.

'Yes.'

'The silent place?'

'The very one,' I said, a little proud he'd caught wind of it. Benny rarely ventured far from his shop, the adjacent grocer's, or The Eagle's Lament over the road.

'I don't think the gays would be much interested in your silent pub,' he said, and I said 'Not at all, Benny, people come in all shapes and sizes, views and outlooks.'

It was *visibility*, I said, which counted over money, or action. Our Instagrammable Rainbow pints would go down a treat with the clientele, the web, the media and, if it so happened, the LGBTQ community.

'Rainbow pints?'

'Aye,' I said.

The hat rack customer played around with some racks, and his homburg. Benny cackled.

'Murphy, you are some prize fool,' said Benny. 'How are you going to layer the food dye so it don't mix together?'

'...'

'Huh?'

'...'

I hadn't thought of that. Had we been stood in The Purser's

Murphy Who Talks

Retainer, the roar and ferocity of Benny's laugh as I walked out would have had him permanently barred from my pub.

'And you mock me for co-opting eastern philosophies' said Rebecca later, stretching, when I told her about Pride, Rainbow Pints, and my plan to be in on the action at The Purser's Retainer so that we weren't visibly outside and therefore off the pulse and out of touch.

'Aye,' I replied, for want of anything better at all.

'You look miserable, Murphy,' she said.

'I am.'

'Why?'

'I think I'm running out of ideas, Rebecca.'

'Eat some more of your Bundt cake,' she said.

I did. The rum tasted like a good use of a wasted day.

I told her I was sad that I'd 'run out of ideas', that the ideas I had come up with were not 'paying off' as I'd hoped, to which Rebecca said 'How so?' and I said, 'I don't know. I guess working at a pub where all talking is banned didn't pan out the way I had in mind'.

Smiling curtly, she asked me why.

'I never wanted door codes,' I said. 'Never wanted to be an exclusive gaff of a place. Never wanted it to be so quiet that I ended up meditating on the meaning of existence between a Jantex spray and a pint of Three or Four.'

'No, you just wanted a bit of peace and quiet.'

'Exactly,' I said.

'Which is the last thing you needed.'

'Oh?'

'You can't have your cake and eat it,' said Rebecca. 'People are annoying, but loneliness is intolerable.'

I swear to Christ, her cake line is a coincidence, a thing that simply came from the unconscious mind. But a novel is a beautiful thing, where anything can happen at all; dots may be jotted by chance, dreams made and come to pass, and men of loss can fall in love and keep it that way. But even novels have their limits, or at the least I was or am of the mind to apply some, for honesty's sake.

I thought then, of telling Rebecca words she'd ordered I not, words that'd 'ruin it', whatever it was between us. But I kept them to myself, shoved a slice of Bundt cake in my vacant maw, watched a little telly, made a little love, and drifted off 'neath a hot July night's heat, knowing that by and large Rebecca was right, silence was not desirable most of the time.

That night, however, with unwarranted pity, she didn't force words from me, much as she'd said she would, didn't make me dive deep or even hover around.

We had talked about it a little the previous day, I had, as they say, 'opened up.'

But that night, she let me off the hook, given the woes in me.

I can only thank the god-awful heat, her earth-learned grace, or both.

Murphy Who Talks

Chapter Twenty-Four

- *Rebecca announces she needs to go home for a while*
- *Murphy realises he's been wrong about absolutely everything all along, which is nice*
- *Gets a phone call from Con Connelly, who never makes phone calls*

Change is often sudden. That is a trite and obvious thing to say.

This is a novel.

Novels, often enough, are profound and deep, unveiling what you didn't know in yourself or hadn't the words for. Often enough too, they simply leave you screaming No shit Sherlock, such that you feel compelled to throw your book at the wall.

Novels are written by people, and people are human, and both are wont to disappoint from time to time.

A word of warning with this one.

The modern landlord is elusive, ethereal and hands-off, until money is involved.

So, go right ahead and throw this book and that sentence and these lines to your nearest wall, but do pause to think about the thin, cheap, shittiness of that rented space, your damned deposit, and whether my trite words make the loss worthwhile.

It was 21:42.

That scorching hot summer could have been a toil for me, with its heat, and its promise, the parks filled with people, the optimism rising up then settling in the hot, fetid air.

To the lonely, warm weather is a mirror of all they lack, be it love, family, friends or just company to pass the time.

I had walked the same streets of North-East London before, a wanting. *I* had been lonely in London.

We're legion so, in that city, veering from one another like negative magnets; through fear, habit, god knows.

But that summer, I'd Rebecca.

The World Cup was a cipher for all that pent-up, emotional labour, and it was a distraction from the chaos, confusion and loss that life had piled upon me.

Football, in all its complexity, had served me well; dulling my senses to the moments that defined me; John Snr's death, Uncle Billy's porridge and the reasons I was there making it, Prague, Karolina; my falls, recoveries, relapses, and the last recovery that fooled the one person who saw through me; my mother.

The World Cup could have distracted me, as the pub and its silence did a while, and I might have muddled along, getting on with the getting on of things.

But I would never have faced it all, were it not for Rebecca. She had me talk as never before; honestly.

She didn't force but she did insist. Didn't criticise but had a way to question and encourage. Didn't judge, but let it be known when my words, actions, evasions or inactions raised eyebrows.

Murphy Who Talks

I loved her for it.

So when change came, and she told me she was leaving, I can without evasion, lie or the *runaround* say I'd plans to talk about it, the one thing that is, that Rebecca had given me licence not to talk about, what with it being fresh, confused and beautifully raw: Mammy, Mum, Mother. We had spoken of it briefly, without diving deep.

Talking's healthy Murphs, done the right way ;) xx
It was 21:44.
I was in her room. She'd her back to me, and her eyes on the laptop screen.

'I'm going home,' she said.
'Righty-oh.'
'For a few days.'
'Sounds lovely,' I said. 'What's the occasion? Aldeburgh Bull Run? Land Rover Rally? Suffolk Drill Festival?'

Rebecca turned and smiled lightly. 'My mum.'
'Ah.'

She brushed cake crumbs off the desk. The sound of a Nissan Believer pierced the whirring fan and the fetid evening air. I asked if it was 'the diabetes'; Rebecca said 'No.'

'I'd just like to see her,' she said.

I nodded. England had beaten the Swedes and were off to the semi-finals. The streets outside were filled with beeps, cheers, noise, the sun was about to give up another evening's ghost.

'Murphy?

I was distracted, not by football, nor thoughts of my ailing and all-too silent pub, but by three letters on my phone, which never appeared there in the form of a call.

Con.

It was my turn to raise an eyebrow, but I ignored it for

now, and turned back to Rebecca.

'You should go see her,' I said. 'She'd love to have you around for a few days.'

Cars, blessed cars, honked angrily at one another in the street, punctuating the fetid, sticky and silent air. Rebecca smiled at me sadly.

'Or weeks,' I said. 'Or however long it is you need to go. She'll be delighted to have you home. We'll chat about my own mother when you're back in London.' She nodded. 'We'll make a plan, so,' I said. 'For the August Bank Holiday?'

Rebecca nodded.

'We could go to a concert.'

'They're very loud,' said Rebecca. 'Will you be able to manage that?'

More cars beeped, more air hung heavy, hot, sticky and still, Rebecca's fan whirred.

'Oh, I'll be grand,' I said, said too 'Go spend a little time with your mum.'

There was no option for silence that night, with the celebratory sounds in the streets, the fan in her room, the low tinkle of music she had on in the background, Fleetwood Mac this time. But it may as well have been silence, for the length of it, unpunctuated as we took to staring at one another.

'til 21:47.

My phone buzzed again. I looked down.

It was Con.

'I had best get this,' I said, to which Rebecca said yes though only with a nod.

'Hello, there, Con Boy.'

'Jesus.'

'Close,' I said. 'Murphy. What's up?'

He was out of breath, like he'd been running, or climbing

a steep set of stairs.

'Christ, Murph,' he said. 'We thought you were dead.'

A Skoda Harmonica whistled in my ears, other vehicles besides.

'Eh? No, I'm fine. What in the name of God are you talking about Con?'

He told me then about The Purser's, the police tape, the body loaded into the ambulance, and how the pair of them had just come across the scene with no clue as to which or whose body was 'neath the sheet, such that they'd a terrifying worry that it might be me.

'I'll be there right away,' I said.

I hung up.

'What's wrong?' said Rebecca.

'There's been some incident up at The Purser's. Ambulances, police, all sorts. I'd best go see what's happened.'

I put on my blue denim jeans, my white shirt, my red shoes.

She stood up. She stroked my hair a moment, gave us a kiss, and sent me on my way.

It was 21:49.

Stephen was alive. Mr. Handley too. And so was I.

As I walked towards the pub, I'd an inkling as to why Con and Don had reason for concern. There were several police cars. There had been an ambulance. The pub was surrounded by police tape, cops urging passers-by to jog on, not gawp, which explained why Con and Don were doing just that from the other side of the road. They saw me approach and walked over.

'Where have you been?' said Don, as I answered through the muffle of a hug.

'Weren't you working?' said Con, and I said 'No' and he said 'But you told us you were' and I said 'Ah' and he looked at me quare and I've to admit I may have given the pair of them reason to think I'd run into a mischief.

I had decided not to watch the game with them, said I was working, and not answered Don's calls or Con's texts 'til the phone had rung.

The death of a lie.

I pointed to the pub, said 'What's happened?', to which Con said 'There was a stabbing. We were walking home this way when we saw the ambulance and police.'

'Christ almighty,' I said. 'Mr. Handley? Stephen?'

'No, said Donnelly. 'It was a kid from the estate over the road. Dead.'

He pointed to the ageing, crumbling place beside the Grayling, where lives were lived.

It was the sort of death that might get into the papers, a half page perhaps. If it'd been me, I've a mind to think, if we're being honest, it'd have gotten more coverage, in the broadsheets and the tabloids, on ITN and the BBC News.

The lights changed; the street open again now, the kid's death stopping traffic for a grand total of thirty-odd minutes. Too black to matter, as the local paper would soon reveal. A good kid, as they are always wont to stress, as if it's just good kids and not the mad city that's the issue at heart.

Honda Cyrillics, Ford Ginas, Volvo Elasticas, they streamed past, filled with owners gawping at the gruesome scene in front of them.

'You two okay?' I said, not knowing whether The Purser's was closed, or if it now simply had the air of a furtive speakeasy, a pastiche of the thing I had wanted it to be.

A while later, looking at my phone, a message from Stephen told me he'd closed the pub that night, on police orders, had not seen what had happened, but recognised *the kid*.

But right then, the pair of them in front of me had the

Murphy Who Talks

same expression of shock and relief, 'til Donnelly said 'So you weren't working?' and I had to say 'No'.

'I was at a girl's house,' I said, and went on to explain how I'd been 'hanging out with a woman named Rebecca' who I met at the yoga, their expressions more elasticated than I ever was.

Donnelly nodded.

'A yoga teacher. Nice.'

The lights went red again. The police spoke on walkie talkies.

Rebecca, I imagined, was still in her room, where I had agreed that yes, it would be healthy to talk about my mum with someone I knew, or not, or maybe even her.

'Why didn't you tell us?' said Con.

I sighed the sigh of a fool who knows his reasons if not his self. Or perhaps now I did.

'Didn't want to jinx a good thing, lads,' I said. 'I've been lonely. It's been nice not to be alone. And I was of a mind not to fuck it up by speaking it aloud if you get me?'

Con looked at me oddly. 'You are one weird cat.'

A car honked, hours now since England had won its game.

'Absolutely.'

Another stream of traffic passed us by. I looked at the pub, then back at the pair of them standing in front of me.

'Will we wander up to The Mother Red Cap to steady your nerves boys?' I said, to which the pair of them there said yes and, as we walked, I wrote to Rebecca to say *There was a stabbing near the pub. The boys feared it was me at first. They're a little shook up. I'm going to take them for a pint if that's alright?*

She replied in an instant, said *yes of course*, said too *hope they're both okay*, said also *text me later, I might have drifted off but I'll try not to.*

She added a smiley face, three kisses besides, and I

remembered that last silence, of sorts, that I broke for her in that room.

'You should spend as much time with your mother as you can, Rebecca. I've been a husk of a man since my Mum died.'

I am not sure she would have been so forgiving of my Freudian slip – it was on the nose to say the least – had my mother been alive, but I imagine the mixed-up texts were passed off as the consequence of muddled thinking, my general clumsiness and, most of all, the delayed grieving which Rebecca was so keen for me to do.

But my mother was dead and had been the length of this tale and earlier. I'd simply been holding on to the only thing I had left of her; the words.

Murphy Who Talks

Chapter Twenty-Five – July

(Zero Months Before)

- *The lads go to Ireland*
- *Murphy goes to Cashel*
- *Murphy goes to The Kingdom*
- *Our bit-this, bit-that, full-this, full-that narrator tries to spell Ó Conghaile without checking Google, and fails*

It was 11:42.

'Murphy.'

'John boy.'

'Con Connelly.'

'John Murphy.'

'Declan.'

'…'

'I said Declan.'

'I heard you, Johnny.'

My brother, the only man who could make Don Donnelly lose the power of words. I loved him for it.

'How's your mum? John Jnr.' asked Con, to which Con said 'Very well' and then 'same old joker' after John Jnr., said 'And Billy?' who was, and remains, Con's father.

'Brilliant stuff,' said my brother John, John Jnr., or Little

John as he was often known, at six foot and one, thirty-seven years of age besides.

'How's the folks?' he asked Donnelly.

'Very well.'

'And the litter?'

Don's was a large family.

'All good,' said Donnelly, and John Jnr. said 'Good', and it was good.

Those were the pleasantries.

It was 11:43.

We'd to be getting on with the getting on of things.

In this instance, the getting on with the getting on of things was the scattering of my mother's ashes.

Yes, Mum was no longer with us.

Those messages between us? Remnants; seconds, minutes, hours even, wasted, scrolling up and down so I could have her back again, a ghost in WhatsApp form.

Let's call a thing a thing the way Donnelly would a girl a girl or a pint a pint. I was dishonest. Led you to believe she was *there*, with me *here*, the pair of us texting back and forth in real time. My mother had died in 2017. She had announced she would sell – and did – the house we grew up in the previous year.

'Why?' said Eileen Jnr. at the time. 'I never knew you wanted to live in Ireland again?'

'Well, it'd be nice to be somewhere quieter,' she said.

'What about the gossips? Auntie Sheila?'

'I'll keep them at arm's length. I'll be over to see you just as often as I am now.'

'How?' said my sister, to which I intervened despite my own misgivings to say 'Ryanair's cheaper than National Rail'.

The sale was settled in March 2016, though Mum would

Murphy Who Talks

later say 'Britain' had 'lost the run of itself altogether', the unintended and sudden bigness of our lives a convenient excuse.

She returned to Cashel in November 2016, a town she had left at the age of seventeen; a choice, a half choice, not really a choice at all.

We were born and reared, scolded and cuddled, moulded and muddled and unleashed upon the world, and then my mother went home, in the belief, I believe, that her work was done, and that I would be fine.

I reacted to losing my job and mother by creating *London's First Silent Pub* and taking up Bikram yoga, so the jury's still out as to whether she was right.

It was 11:44 as I thought of this, and we were on the road from Dublin.

Little John had driven us down in his Honda Deux Ex Machina.

We were in the kitchen, heading out for the night to escape the cloying air in mum's house. It smelled of Febreze, reeked of recent death and passing life.

It was 18:04.

We went to Ó Conghaile's, saw my uncle and aunt, ate and drank well.

'John Jnr.'
'Uncle Tom.'
'Murphy.'
'Uncle Tom.'
'Sheila.'
'Lovely to see you boys.'
'This is Con Connelly and Declan Donnelly.'
'Like the lad off ITV?'

Don pursed his mouth, John Jnr., said 'The very one,' with

a needling glint in his eye.

'Welcome to Cashel boys, it's lovely to see you all,' said Uncle Tom. 'What are you drinking?'

It was 18:23.

We ordered Heineken, Guinness, Guinness and Heineken, Sheila had a large glass of Sauvignon Blanc, and Uncle Tom got himself a pint of Harp and throughout the night spoke of my mother, the country losing the run of itself, the hurling season, the football season, the soccer season, and everything else besides.

'til around three in the morning.

It was 10:01.

We hit the road.

That was Cashel.

And this was the Kingdom. County Kerry. Land of my father.

It was 13:06.

For all his flaws, Don Donnelly had booked the flights months earlier, insisting he would 'see the old girl off', and while I knew my mother would have turned in her grave to be described as such had she not been cremated, was grateful all the same.

Con offered to come as well.

So, the messages, between myself and Mum?

Women don't have counties, Murphy.
I'm after being ticked off by the guards.
Your Uncle Michael was in town earlier
Will you be watching the game?

Nostalgia. It was part of my routine. Cleaning shelves, making coffee, checking to see if I'd the cancer, inspecting the Jackson-Pollock-coagulate in my tissues after sneezing first thing of a morning.

It became a part of my day, to read through old messages, chase fragments of her, scroll over anything I did not like to read or dwell on.

Does it not get a bit lonely over there? written, my own misgivings alluded to, why did you leave me behind thought; unsaid.

Mum went to Ireland not knowing she'd the cancer. Knowing might have altered her plans. The day I rang to say I'd lost my job, she said, was the same day she had planned on telling me of the diagnosis.

'Are you okay?' I said, after answering her call. She'd a rare deadness in her voice.

'I'm fine, I'm fine. Now, explain to me what happened with the job.'

'The magazine went under.'

'Any reason why?'

'Qatar had a spat with the Emirates over oil.'

'Any resolution in the pipeline?'

'No, it's the pipeline that's dried up. They've had to make cuts.'

'I'm sorry.'

'Me too.'

And that was that, for another week or so.

When she told Eileen Jnr., Eileen Jnr. told me, and when I spoke to Mum she'd a light optimism in her voice, shooing away our fears the way mothers do, with words like 'good prognosis' and 'caught early' and claims as to the best oncologists in Dublin being involved.

And I'm sure it was true, they were very good oncologists, only it turned out the cancer was very good at its job too.

I was there near the end. Read to her. Sat with her, what was left of her. Then she passed.

There was a funeral. A cremation in Cork. A wake in Tipperary. Uncle Tom bought the rounds. There was a drive back to Dublin with my siblings. A night with John Jnr. at his flat, a no-frills Ryanair flight, a hug to Eileen Jnr. and an 'I'm expecting again' before we said goodbye.

And then I moved out of one flat and into another, on the Lorraine Estate.

We each of us got on with things in our own way. My sister sued her university for discrimination, her body swelled. My brother buried himself in work. I sat on my arse, trying but not trying, to find it and then I did, and that was the state of the Murphy clan at the start of this tale.

There are worse families. Klans too, for that matter.

It was 13:15.

It was 18:04.

We'd dropped off our stuff and wandered into town.

'You're English I presume?'

'Not at all.'

'Welsh?'

'Absolutely not, sir.'

'Ye don't sound American.'

'I did a season Bitcoin mining in Wisconsin, sir, on a working visa. I am not from the USA.'

The barman looked confused. 'Well you're definitely not an Irishman.'

Don Donnelly had a nice little giggle at that.

'We're from London,' I said.

'So you *are* English?'

'No, we're London Irish.'

The barman scoffed. 'Like the rugby team?'

'Aye.'

Murphy Who Talks

'Right-oh,' he said, placing the last pint on the counter.
'What's the damage?'
'€22.60.'
I whistled. 'Irish prices.'
'Worse than London Irish prices?'
'No, but close enough.'
'Are London Irish prices the same as London London prices?'
'No,' I said, resigned, admitted they were 'more or less the same'.
I paid the man. He smiled.

John Jnr. supped his pint, beigey foam on the designer-Dublin-stubble of his upper lip whiskers.
'Our father was born up the road.'
The barman looked at the doorway, past which was *up the road*. 'Where?' he said.
'In the hospital,' said John Jnr. 'The one that's now the AIB.'
The barman nodded.
'I was born in the very same place. What's his name?'
'John Murphy.'
The barman nodded. 'I knew him.'
'Yes?'
'Yes.'
John Jnr. nodded.
'He went missing at sea, did he not?'
'He did, yeah.'
'Was he ever found?'
'He wasn't, no.'
The barman nodded one last time.
'Oh well.'
He smiled, lightly, like he knew us a little, or was just

decent, or a little of both.

'Welcome home, lads.'

'Thanks.'

And that was us home. The Belgians played the French. The Belgians lost one to nil.

'Do you think it'll happen?' the barman asked a while after the Belgians had lost to France.

Connelly said 'I guess', Donnelly 'It can't', Little John 'It mustn't', me 'It will and it must but I wish that it wouldn't'.

The barman nodded. 'It'll be a disaster, I'd say.'

As a collective we agreed that yes, it would, and ordered another drink.

Later, when it was quieter, the barman spoke to us more.

We told him about Mum's passing. Condolences were offered.

We told him she was from Tipperary, he asked why we were scattering her *here* not *there*.

'She liked Kerry,' I said, to which he said ''tis beautiful when you stop to look at it' and John Jnr. added 'She liked coming here,' and, 'She was sentimental in her own way'.

The barman smiled glintingly.

'Ah look it, that's beautiful is it not?' he said, and we agreed it was, and he stood us another round on the house.

It was 22:03.

We had decided on a July scattering as August forever disappointed, its expected sun often subsumed 'neath rain and wind, and Eileen Jnr. had told us that we ought to go ahead with it now and delay no further, as the time was right and she was too close to term, and I came to think that the two things were conveniently placed and couldn't blame her for wanting to stay clear. Deep down, she was a little angry with Mum, I'd

Murphy Who Talks

say, for having left England in the first place.

As was I, though I'd a mind to understand she had her reasons.

It was 22:41.

The barman had settled in for a late night conversation.

'Where are you going to scatter her ashes?'

'Skellig Michael,' said Little John.

Skellig Michael is an island twelve kilometres off the west coast. Monks lived there in the 13th century. Seals and lots of birds too. It's a nature reserve, and was a quiet enough beauty spot, 'til a *Star Wars* filming crew came to town. The tourists came in droves. The local economy got a huge boost. That's show business.

The barman looked aghast, impressed, mortified and amused.

'Out of the question,' he said. 'It's a nature reserve. There'd be hell to pay.'

Rules are rules.

'I know,' I said, and John Jnr. said 'We know' and Don Donnelly said 'They got engaged there,' and the barman said 'Ah, that's lovely'.

'My cousin operates boat trips there and back. Booked through 'til September,' he said, said too he'd 'give him a buzz', and noted that for two fifty euro notes the cousin might shift things about and also turn a blind eye.

Brilliant stuff.

It was 23:22.

Chapter Twenty-Six

- *His part-time Dacency, Man*
- *Murphy tells Rebecca about the letter*
- *Mum and Murphy have words, spoken, read too*

I wasn't living in the flat on the Lorraine Estate when Mum died, though it wasn't her dying that made me the nervous, tiptoe type either, I was like that before; furtively moving around spaces rented with strangers, worried I was in the way, trying to stay out of the way.

I had lived in a place called 55a, with three lads who – on all their days – were like Don on his most hard-nosed days; cunt and tits the worst of it, fanny the best, like.

I did not like them, nor their Janus-faced decency when my mother died, a decency that betrayed the bit black, bit white, no, full black-and-white thinking I'd developed of them, to see myself as better, to believe if a cunt of a man was a cunt of a man he was a cunt and nothing more; good, bad, in between at various times.

They offered to be stand up men in a time of crisis, when, I'd say, what we sorely needed was for men to be as such; always, quietly.

*

Murphy Who Talks

My mother wrote me a letter. When I moved to the Lorraine Estate, I left it unopened on a shelf, balanced delicately against four books, a Sauron with neatly curled handwriting.

Months I left it there, and after Rebecca mooted the idea of me writing a letter to my mother, I'd to admit that if I did it'd be a case of writing back, only I'd to read what she had to say first.

It was the second surprise of a scorching hot afternoon, wherein I'd had to admit Mum had not only moved back to Ireland permanently, but that yes, she had passed also, just like my Dad, a revelation Rebecca found surprising, several weeks into whatever it was we had; a relationship, a sort of relationship, no relationship at all.

With grace, and tact, she said she understood my not telling her the full truth, though of course she couldn't and I was glad.

The letter. She was surprised I'd yet to read it.

'What? You haven't?'

'No.'

'Are you not curious?'

'As George.'

'What?'

'It's an American cartoon about a monkey. I'm hoping for a US audience.'

'Eh?'

'Nothing,' I said. 'I'll read it one of these days.'

She would have curled a lock of my hair in her fingers then, only I hadn't enough of it to curl, so she just stroked my temple instead.

'There might be instructions for buried treasure,' I said, after a while.

'Or a recipe for apple pie.'

'My mother didn't bake.'

'Ah.'

A Honda Scalextric broke up the dialogue.

'Was your mother in the habit of burying treasure, Murphy?'

'She wasn't, no.'

'If it were my mother, I'd be keen to see what she had to say.'

And I was.

So I did, in my own time.

'Murphy, love.'

I peered from the window of the house my mother had moved into, staring at the Rock of Cashel in the distance, convincing myself her reasons for moving home were just. I could see a cluster of people moving around the fields ahead, American tourists I'd say. Hadn't she more cherished memories of us, in England, than her youth, here?

'Yes?' I said, turning to look at her.

Her skin was grey like a seal's, and she was thin, as she had always been until her early fifties, when she had begun to put on a healthy amount of middle-aged, female fat.

There are reasons why men should not write about women's bodies, in novels, or at all.

Her eyes were sunken, lips colourless. She could no longer read much, only a little, eyes failing her, mind too. Though she found it hard to concentrate on anything for prolonged periods of time, she could still hold court. She smiled.

'You were quiet as a mouse.'

'Me?'

She laughed, cancerally.

'Yes. The midwife said you were the quietest baby she'd ever seen.'

Murphy Who Talks

She lifted herself a little on the bed. 'Did I ever tell you we left the hospital the same day you were born?'

'No,' I said, only she had, fifty or maybe a hundred times or more. 'Wasn't that John Jnr?' I said, thinking it smart, that she might then tell the story for her own satisfaction.

Only she looked confused then, wondering, cancerally, if she'd mixed the pair of us up after all. But she furrowed her brow, with a determined expression.

'No, it was yourself. John Jnr. mewled like a cat, then went quiet after your father died. You were the other way around.'

I nodded.

'Didn't you say I'd lots of hair?'

She laughed. 'I did. You were fair headed like your father and liked to stare.'

'How old was I when I first spoke?'

'Eleven months,' she said.

My sister thought it ten, said it was *Eila* I'd said first, to her, only my mother convinced herself it was *gaga* or *iya* so she could claim the hearing of my first word herself; apple.

There was a short and rare silence, before she next spoke.

'I wouldn't have moved back had I known what would happen.'

'With the illness?' I said, to which she smiled, said 'That? No. With your job.'

'Oh, that. I'm fine,' I said, and she smiled, wan, as an Opal Missive clogged along on the nearest main road. 'I will be,' I said. 'Don't worry.'

I'd say it was like asking a chimpanzee not to fart and eat, sleep and screw.

I looked out of the window, felt her cold hand on my arm and looked around. She smiled, made to say something, only said instead after some difficulty, 'Read to me a while'. This all happened before I met Rebecca West and discovered honesty.

But words read worked for me and my mother, well enough, so I read, and she listened, and the pair of us enjoyed each other's company while we could.

Don Quixote, sweating eyes edition.

Murphy Who Talks

Chapter Twenty-Seven

- *The boys scatter Eileen Murphy's ashes on Skellig Michael, a big island*
- *A sailor lets Murphy wear his hat*
- *An incident involving puffins, peril, and sweating eyes*
- *England play a football game at the FIFA World Cup*

The ineffable pull of home drew my mother back to Cashel from London the way London pulled me from Prague. We've each our own delusions.

In the year or so after her death, I'd my own, burying myself in work, football, the *runaround*, and it was Rebecca who forced me to confront the matter.

She was wrong about the letter though. It said little that wasn't said that Tuesday afternoon in Cashel. Mum was of the mind that writers write, painters paint, nurses nurse and hurlers hurl.

She left each to do their own, and as such her letter was to the point.

Dear Murphy,

You're a good man, and a kind fool. I love you very much. Take care of your siblings and yourself. Let love and pain in. Talk about it. Grieve and grow. Keep writing your books. Read them too.

Mum

You think me flippant?
Bongo.

It was 10:42.

We were in Portmagee, a small fishing village on the chin of the Irish coast; responsible for two of my grandparents, and a frequent contender in Ireland's Tidy Towns award.

Twelve kilometres in the distance are Skelligs Michael and Bheag. One had the monks and *Star Wars*, the other a colony of gannet birds.

We were heading Michael's way, on the boat, ready to head out, the barman's cousin, the boatman, readying the vessel, tickling the hawser's, proofreading the sandwiches, checking the cash-in-hand payment (plus standard Skellig Michael transfer fee) so we could be on our way.

'You're from England?' he said.

'Positively so, sir.'

'Where?'

'London town.'

'My brother lives there.'

'Whereabouts?'

'Elephant and Castle,' said the boatman, and I dipped my hand in the water, raised it like a tusk, and 'sprayed it' in Connelly's hung-over face.

Murphy Who Talks

Four of us had a nice little giggle at that. Connelly weighed it up, decided the unpleasant surprise was refreshing, on balance, and, after the night before, welcome too. I was glad to help.

We'd bribed the boatman. We set sail. We were on our way. The boatman let me wear his hat.

It was 11:42. We had docked, we had begun to walk up a steep set of steps laid by monks centuries before.

'Do you know any songs Mum liked?' I asked.

'Plenty,' said John Jnr. 'She liked Fleetwood Mac.'

'Whack on 'Songbird' will you Con?' I said.

He did. Or tried. Accidentally put on 'Don't Stop' instead. It was a little light for the occasion.

It was 11:46 too.

We were halfway up the steps, nearing the place at which our mother requested we set her to the wind. We were nearly *there*, only we were still *here*, and something happened in between.

A puffin.

'...'

It was 11:47.

'Murphy, don't blame yourself,' said John Jnr.

'I didn't think puffins moved that fast,' said Con Connelly.

Don said he had not seen one before, save for on the 'Guinness ad'. I stared down the steep green and rocky incline, towards the rocks, the sea, at the puffins gathered below, pecking away at the ashes of my mother.

'That's a toucan,' said John Jnr. 'It's not the same.'

Donnelly nodded then, like the rest of us, looked down, and stared.

*

Monks aside, the island is home to thousands of puffins, a small and stupid but pretty bird. They move, as Con said, quickly, and one had fizzled by my ear as we walked, causing me to drop the urn, which fell towards the rocks, opening – thankfully – just as it rolled to what now seemed her final place of rest.

The puffins pecked away as we continued to stare. I felt a hand on my shoulder. It was John. Jnr.

'I think maybe we'd best cut our losses,' he said. 'We still managed to sc–'

He had turned to me mid-sentence, cutting himself short at the sight of my sweating eyes. 'Murphy, you did your best to make it nice. She'd find it funny.'

I looked down. Puffins, pecking at my mother's remains. He wasn't wrong, she would as well. But funny had to come after. Without funny there was no point, only I was of the view that without serious a moment, there was no point in funny either, such that that and this and this and that had to complement each other.

Looking back at him, I shook my head lightly.

'No,' I said. 'We've to do it the right way.'

He nodded. I walked down the steps, off-track, onto the mossy, acidic grass and earth.

Had one of them said 'Don't, Murphy' or 'It's not allowed, Murphy' or 'You fool, Murphy!, it's a €800 fine,' I might have taken hold of what little senses I had left. But they didn't, so I walked, footfalls heavy on the green grass, the acidic bog soil of West Kerry firm beneath my fingers as I used it to guide myself down, reaching the puffins and the fallen urn.

'Shoo!' I said, and the five of them scattered.

The urn had a fracture on its metal base, but was otherwise intact, Mum on the ground, not-on the ground, a bit of both. I

Murphy Who Talks

scooped up what I could and let the lapping waves do the rest.

That was fine.

I turned around and looked up at John. He nodded at me to continue, so I looked out towards the sea a moment and said a couple of words that were mine and hers and not yours to hear.

And then I scattered and watched and had the experience of wind sending a bit of my mother's ashes back into my eyes and mouth.

Funny.

I went back to my brother and my friends.

A man on the trail called me out for my 'utter stupidity' and 'illegal' behaviour.

'Sir?' I said.

'What?'

'I just scattered my mam's ashes. Get fucked, sir.'

I turned to the boys, standing just slightly behind me. 'Let's go find the boatman.'

We'd a game to watch in the evening; England, dicking around with Croatia, on a green rectangle in Moscow.

'That was quick,' said the boatman, when we met him.

'Aye, it was,' I said. 'You'll be back in time for lunch.'

It was 11:55.

I hadn't heard from Rebecca since arriving in Ireland, nor her me, and so I was unsure which of us was waiting to receive a one-tick grey message that would then go two-tick blue.

Had I truly wanted to, I could have broken the digital silence. But I feared there was a chance that with the supposed safety of distance I might say or at least hint I was in love with a mixture of emojis maybe, and some choice words. So instead, I decided to leave her to her mother a while, and she to mine, and got on with the getting on of things in County Kerry instead.

It was a hot evening, sun shining on the Celtic pub fronts. We were in O'Sullivan's, and it was quiet. I thought of the noise, life and clamour of the pubs in London, wondered what I was missing, more inside of things all along than I had realised.

I wondered about that hider's place, The Purser's Retainer, co-opted now, where forgotten ones went. I thought of The Regional Pickpocket, its life, youth and clamour, and looked around the pub with its Gaelic football photos, and felt as home in one as the other, alright being *here*, knowing I could go back *there* in good time and hadn't to fight for *here* as mine anymore.

The game began.

'Good luck, so!' said a man at the bar.

The four of us nodded. We watched. England lost, and that was the end of that.

It'd been a fun few weeks for everyone. Distracting. Binding. Pointless. Better than hate, hunger or war. There was that.

It was 21:23.

Murphy Who Talks

Chapter Twenty-Eight

- *The Purser's Retainer goes out in style*
- *Vegan meat raffle*
- *The FIFA World Cup 2018 comes to an anticlimactic close*

———

It was 9:44.

I got up, swung my legs round and placed the feet on the floor. Ach-oo, ach-oo, ach-oo, the daily sneezes came. I reached for the tissue, unleashed fury into a two-ply, checked the damage. Little bit of snot, only a capillary's worth of blood. Not much chance of the cancer, I'd say.

Getting up, I threw the tissue in the bin, and knocked my knee on the edge of my bed.

'Frigid fetlocks!'

No sound from Juliette as of yet, so I'd a moment's concern for the noise I made. Did I still worry? Yes. A little.

I made a breakfast. Two eggs. A little bread. Some butter.

It was hot as hell out, still, and it was as if the World Cup was over, even though the final was yet to be played. People were glum again on the buses and trains and in cars and walking on streets, or it seemed so.

I hadn't been back to yoga since my return, had written to Rebecca to say *Ireland was fine, fine god awfully fine how's you?* to which she'd said *fine, been a bit of a mad week* and I wrote back only *I hope it's all okay.*

There was no reply, and I'd work at eleven.

There was the getting on of getting on with things to be getting on with.

I punched in the new keycode. 1984.

It opened, but there was no one inside, Stephen having cottoned onto the fact that for all of this and that, that and this, I was responsible enough to wipe the shelves, apply the taps, turn on the lights, sweep the floors, shuffle the menus, feed the mice and get the bar ready for the day.

And yet there he was, a moment later, walking through the backroom door.

'Ah, Murphy.'

'Stephen.'

'How was Ireland?'

'...green.'

A Mitsubishi Memphis moaned past the window, its exhaust on the troubled side.

'I'll make it there one of these days,' he said.

I wasn't so sure, said nothing, and made to get on with the sweeping, which I liked to do first thing, followed by the bar lights, the shelves, the mice.

But Stephen was there to stop me.

'I've a little bit of bad news, Murphy.'

'The cancer?'

'No.'

'The clap?'

He looked at me, cock-eyed, and rolled out an elongated 'No'.

'Don't tell me Thatcher's back?'

'No,' he said, then 'Not yet'.

Murphy Who Talks

We both had a nice little giggle at that.

Stephen looked at me sadly, beads of nervous sweat pooling on his balding head, his short-sleeved shirt sodden already 'neath July's unremitting heat.

'We're closing,' he said.

'The pub?'

'Yes.'

'Because of the stabbing?' I said. 'Are we a crime scene now? Should I have come in through the back door? I hope I've not contaminated anything.'

Stephen laughed. 'No, Murphy. That's old news.'

I'd say I was on the verge of a rant then, as he lifted a finger so I would let him speak.

'The CPO didn't go our way,' he said. 'The pub's being sold. I'm selling up. Which means...'

'No more pub.'

'Pretty much,' said Stephen.

I picked up a menu. It was flecked with the sauce off of our jerk colcannon, a bit of ketchup too.

'Is there nothing we can do?' I said. 'A quiz for Syria? Gaga for Gaza? Bikram Jenga?'

'Murphy.'

'Arses for Sweden?'

'*Murphy*. I don't think that would work.'

Neither did I, but it was worth a go.

'The CPO was always going to win. The building is crumbling at the rafters. I knew full well when you started here, we only had a year tops. I'm sorry, I should have been more up front.'

'But I thought you wanted to fight the CPO?'

He shook his head. 'To be honest with you, it was just a bit of fun, letting you do your thing; your schemes and ideas, your phone ban.'

'It wasn't a ban.'
'Your phone ban that wasn't a ban.'
'Good man.'

He looked out of the window, so that the dialogue might be broken up a line.

'The silent pub,' he said. 'Even I got caught up in that one.'
'You did indeed.'
'It was a hoot, alright. It was, what's that phrase of yours. The craic?'

Close enough, I thought, and sat at the bar, hunched over by nature, his news too. 'Absolutely.'

I looked around. I would miss it, so. 'May I pour myself a pint Stephen?' I asked.

He looked at his watch, lifted an eyebrow, and shrugged. 'I can't see why not.'

'And a crafty snout?'

He nodded, said 'Be my guest' and, symbolically, slid a pint glass with a dreg's worth of water in it towards me, a receptacle for the ash.

I pushed the boat out and poured myself a pint of Six.

'I'm sorry I lied to you, Murphy,' he said, after I'd let the pint settle and topped it up. 'It seemed like a welcome distraction from everything else you had going on. You looked like a man enjoying life.'

I sat at the bar, a railbird in the same uniform I wore the other side of it, in my room, talking to Juliette, scattering my mother, dating in The Olive Branch, shoulder-hunch drinking in Erin's Rejoinder, trying its opposite in The Regional Pickpocket, everywhere else besides. I smiled.

'Absolutely, Stephen,' I said. 'Absolutely.'

I exhaled, a plume of blue, delicious, cancerous smoke. A Nissan Fictitia pootled by.

Murphy Who Talks

'What will you do now?'

A Toyota Tamagotchi beeped at a poor old Mini Fat Controller.

'I'll get by,' I said.

The lights turned red. The clock behind the bar had been wrong since before the day I had first arrived.

'Sounds good, Murphy,' said Stephen.

The air was very still, the only sounds made-up cars, beeped horns, the destitute wandering the streets, and a man shouting on his phone.

'Stephen?'

'Yes, Murphy?'

'Can we have a closing party?'

'We can,' he said. He laughed. 'A quiet one. No party poppers.'

I smiled, lifted my eyes and fixed them to the pumps of Three and Eight, Two and Four, which hadn't been aligned in chronological order, with life so very upside down.

'No,' I said, shaking my head. 'To hell with that.'

'What?'

I looked at him.

'Silence,' I said. 'I'm sick to the teeth of it. Let's go out with a racket.'

We showed the World Cup final. France Croatia. Four goals to two. The tournament went out with a whimper, as parties often do. Like it or not, I'd wanted England there, at the last. The England I wanted had never and did not exist, which is not to say I didn't dream that one day it might.

When the football was done, we drank, and sang, and danced; Con Connelly, Donnelly, Stephen, even Mr. Handley too.

What would happen to him now? I'd the impression he

was sadder than his aged and failing eyes let on. There were other pubs, of course, where he could drink his pints, read his damned *Express*, express his views, but it wouldn't be the same, I knew.

We drank, and sang, and danced.

The homeless (people) reappeared – bar Jack – and partied, were fed to the gills with gin and whiskey, porter and pints, though not wine, as none of them had a liking for it, save for Jack, who was in a shelter, or had been relocated, or was in birdy, or was dead.

No one knew.

We drank, and sang, and danced. We made a hell of a racket. We made a hell of a noise.

On our last Monday we did karaoke. On the Tuesday, a vegan meat raffle to give Mr. Handley one last go of the *runaround*. On the Wednesday we did a quiz. Answers were debated. Mine – as quizmaster – were final.

On the Thursday we did nothing special, and on Friday we drank, and sang, and danced the one last time.

'What are you going to do next, Murphy?' said Mr. Handley, sat in his chair.

'I'll dance,' I said. 'And then I'll find a new job.'

He nodded. 'Anything in mind?'

I shrugged. 'Another pub. Writing again. E-cigarettes.'

'E-cigarettes? Like vaping machines?'

'No,' I said. 'My friend Benny Vape from Mitchem tried to get me into that game. Mucky business. I'm talking about online cigarettes. You sniff the keyboard. Imbibe the nicotine through the web.'

I handed the man his pint.

'Murphy?'

'Yes?'

Murphy Who Talks

'Shut up, Murphy.'
'Yes, Mr. Handley.'
I began to walk.
'Murphy?'
'Yes, sir?'
'Good luck.'
'Thank you, muchly, Mr. Handley.'

We drank, sang and danced.
And in the morning, I went to meet Rebecca in the park, leaving me only with sweet memories of her room.

Chapter Twenty-Nine

- *Rebecca tells Murphy it's over*
- *Murphy tells Rebecca he's going to stop going to Bikram*
- *Rebecca tells him he should not*
- *Murphy insists he will*
- *Murphy chases a squirrel*

It was 13:03.

The rain had come and gone a couple of times, but it was still boiling hot, trees dappled with unforgiving sun beams that had my white shirt near-sodden with sweat, my flabby cheeks sweltering beneath July's undying light.

It was glorious, only it mightn't have been had I never met her in the first place.

I might've craved identity still, or had another breakdown, or feared I'd the cancer after each morning sneeze with the same severity as before.

'Hello, Murphy,' said Rebecca, to which I said, 'Hello back, it's nice to see you' and she said 'You too.'

We'd a hug.

'How was Ireland?'

'Rainy, windy, pinty, familial. Fine.'

Murphy Who Talks

'Have you spoken to your sister?'

'Aye, I'm going to go up to visit next week. Tell her all about it, see how she's getting on.'

'Good. How was your brother?'

'Little John? Grand.'

'It was nice of your friends to go with you.'

'It was.'

'They sound supportive.'

'They are.'

They were decent enough men, in fairness.

Donnelly would always be a prick, grow out of being a prick, or he'd be a bit of a prick at times, good at times, both, I didn't know.

Con, for his part, would get over Daisy, and meet someone new, or not; he might have a two-up two-down in five years and two kids besides, or his waist might gradually migrate east and west and he'd settle into a bachelordom no one could have predicted when he was a young man in a band, on a stage, singing his heart out, playing his guitar; might become a DJ, a Friday night gun for hire on the small stages in Harrow's various part-Irish, part-English but mostly Irish bars. Who knew?

For now, however, it was me and Rebecca, walking in Finsbury Park, shrouded 'neath its glorious birch trees, walking on the grass.

'I'm going back to Aldeburgh for good, Murphy,' said Rebecca. 'My mum needs me there.'

She stood on a twig, had her hands in her pockets. 'I need me there.'

We walked on silently a moment. I've a memory of saying only 'That'll be good for you both', believe I was stoic, but in truth I must have had the makings of sweating eyes, for she said, 'You'll be okay, Murphy'.

I looked at her. Affable.

'I know.'

A dalmatian with extra spots ran by, its owner after having thrown it its ball. I looked back at Rebecca.

'You'll be fine yourself,' I said. 'Home is home. 'tis good to find it. Besides, there's no shortage of middle class women in Aldeburgh who'd pay good money for yoga classes, I'd say.'

Rebecca shook her head. 'No, there's not.'

'And you'll be nearer to your mother. Away from London, all the noise. It's not for everyone.'

'I will, she said, said too that she didn't think she'd 'be back in London on the August Bank Holiday. But if I am, we'll meet up then? As promised.'

The dalmatian dog ran back to his owner, as I said, 'We will,' said too I hoped it'd 'be a washout so we can go to the pub.'

Rebecca smiled. 'Sounds like a plan. Will you keep going to yoga?' she asked.

'No, I said. 'I think I've had enough of that.'

'You should keep going. You've been getting more flexible.'

'I should probably watch the pennies. The money my mother left me won't last forever, and seventy five quid a month is obnoxious. I'm trying to strengthen my back, Rebecca, not buy cocaine.'

She nodded.

'Fair.'

Sometimes I think that I pedestalled Rebecca, let her fill a void, gave her an unfair burden as consequence. But usually, I conclude that I was good to her, and she me, and I'm glad now it was never said, but we both knew love that summer, in a way.

'It's a nice day out,' I said. 'Shall we go for a walk before you go? The squirrels are out in force.'

Murphy Who Talks

Rebecca smiled. 'Do you want to chase them?'

I did. So we went and did that. Whether they loved or loathed us for it, I couldn't say.

They're squirrels, after all.

Murphy Who Talks

Epilogue

That night I went to the pub, as I had the evening off.
I met Connelly, Don too. They were a little late.
It was 19:46. I read my book.
I got in a Heineken, sat with the book, and was distracted as I read the news on my phone, down a rabbit hole of frustration, confusion, anger, bemusement, pain that could easily become despair.
I had to laugh, if I wasn't to yelp, scream, lash out or cry.
They hadn't a clue. Not a clue what they were doing. I was angry, no, I was sad, not at what they were doing but at what it distracted us from; the art of being human.

We were busy.
Busy falling in and out of love, busy getting jealous and obsessed, hung up, frustrated, mad, loud, angry and sad.
Busy with joy, despondency and confusion too. Busy with excitement and boredom, lousiness, goodness, neediness and being needed also. Busy worrying.
Busily hopeful, despite the distractions on screen and in mind that had you thinking life was big when it was small, that things were simple when they were not.
We were human beings, busy being busy, and we'd to be getting on with the getting on of that.

Acknowledgements

I would like to thank my mother, whose unwavering love and support has seen me through years of uncertainty, mental ill health and the trials and tribulations that come with being a writer. I could not have done it without you, and I love you dearly.

I would like to thank my siblings for their encouragement over the years, and my friends Brian, Freddie and John for their companionship and company in the real-world Purser's and Regional Pickpockets of London.

Special thanks go to Indie Novella for believing in the book and taking a chance on me, particularly Damien; your feedback and insight have been invaluable.

I would also like to thank Rachel Seiffert for encouraging me to pursue this project further in its early stages, and to lean into the themes that had emerged.

Unlike Murphy, I have always valued communication. For me, literature does that and, as such, I want to acknowledge the works of art that influenced me while writing the novel, in the hope that others might seek out and enjoy them too. Paul Beatty's *The Sellout*, Josef Hašek's *The Good Soldier Švejk* and *Don Quixote* rank among the funniest books I have read and were vital texts in helping me shape Murphy as a character. Olivia Sudjic's *Sympathy*, meanwhile, is not only a fantastic novel but a masterclass in characterisation and the exploration of relationship dynamics. And a final literary nod must go to Anna Burns' *Milkman*, its use of language showing me how tone and voice can be used as a narrative device. Finally, I'd like to acknowledge the music of The National, comedy of Bob Mortimer, and the feet of Dele Alli. Art is of many a kind.

Finally, I would like to thank C, for loving me, supporting me, and for believing in me. I love you more than you can imagine.